D1520883

The Runaway
Princess

The Runaway Princess

Carol M. Schede

Five Star • Waterville, Maine

Five Star First Edition Romance Series.

Published in 2001 in conjunction with Carol M. Schede.

Set in 11 pt. Plantin.

Printed in the United States on permanent paper.

Library of Congress Cataloging-in-Publication Data

Schede, Carol M., 1947–
    The runaway princess / Carol M. Schede.
        p. cm.— (Five Star first edition romance series)
    ISBN 0-7862-3321-4 (hc : alk. paper)
    1. Princesses—Fiction. 2. Automobile racing drivers—
Fiction. 3. South Carolina—Fiction. I. Title. II. Series.
    PS3619.C34 R86 2001
    813'.6—dc21   2001023681

With special and loving thanks to
Barbara,
mentor, critiquer, cheerleader, and very dear friend,
and to
Kathy and Dawn,
who have suffered with me through
every single work of every
manuscript I have ever written,
and who never doubted—not even once.

Author's Note

There is no Mediterranean principality of Île d'Arinedra, or a honky-tonk named Cooter's in Atlanta. The author has also taken liberties with the layout of Darlington Raceway in South Carolina, and with the manner in which a professional racecar driver would conduct himself during a race.

Chapter 1

What in the hell is going on over there? Ian Grayson wondered. Somebody was thumping the holy hell out of the wall in the condo next door. And cussing a blue streak. The words were incomprehensible—and strangely exotic—but the inflection was quite clear.

Ian briefly wondered if maybe he ought to check on his neighbor, whoever that might be, but the effort seemed too great. His leg hurt. His back hurt. His head hurt. Besides all that hurting, he was far too recognizable to blunder around attempting good deeds.

A visit over there would also require putting on some pants.

Ian tried to ignore his real reason for not getting involved in whatever strangeness was going on next door—the view that would hit him squarely in the face the minute he opened his own front door. Aside from periodic forays into the outside world for food and liquor, Ian stayed as far away from his front door as possible.

He could sit out on his back balcony and sip whatever he happened to be sipping while he surveyed, six floors beneath him, the wide expanse of white, packed sand that was Daytona Beach. He could watch the ocean come and go, the cars drive up and down the beach when the tide permitted, and whatever the hell else was going on out there while he pretended this was nothing more than a rare day off.

But every time he stepped out on to the covered breezeway outside his front door, great waves of almost-physical pain hit him squarely in the gut. Closely following those waves of pain was a bottomless black hole: his uncertain future. Because rearing its head out of the flat Florida landscape and impossible to miss from six floors up, as he looked west across the Halifax River, there it lurked; taunting him, ridiculing him, probably laughing at him, if the truth be known—the speedway, that big-assed, huge two-and-a-half-mile, high-banked mother—

"What in the *hell* is going on over there?" Ian grunted out loud as something else, this time big and heavy, clattered against the other side of his living room wall. The racket hadn't stopped, nor had the cussing.

A guy plunked down a few hundred thousand dollars for a decent place to hide out in peace and quiet during those several times each year he was required to be in Daytona Beach, and what did he get? No damned peace and quiet, that's for sure!

Ian hobbled off to the bedroom in search of some jeans and a shirt. He was just out of the hospital. Sick. Fragile. Irritated. He needed serenity—and another drink.

What kind of a godforsaken place was this, anyway? How was a guy supposed to indulge in serious self-pity with all that damned commotion over there? It was a terrible nuisance, but it looked as if he would just have to limp over there and set somebody straight.

Katriana Saint Ranganeaux realized that she was congenitally incapable of cooking. It was quite possible that before long she would simply starve to death in this strange country, surrounded by overabundance.

Cooking should be easy—it looked easy on television.

However, until this unfortunate point in her life, Katriana had never given much thought to actual food preparation. At mealtime, food appeared, beautifully presented, prepared and spiced. After the meal, everything disappeared. She had no knowledge of, or interest in, exactly how those meals came to exist.

Until she grew famished and attempted to prepare her own food—alone, hiding out in these strange, dreary, cramped "condominium" accommodations, barely large enough to be decent servants' quarters.

"Merde!" Katriana spat, not for the first time. How hard could it be to cook a potato? Could one not drop it into a pot and somehow cook it in water? But for how long?

Certainly longer than she had allowed on that first try!

She couldn't even spear the impenetrable rock of a potato with the big, evil-looking fork, now clutched in her hand. She knew quite well how improper it was to spear one's food, but starvation called for desperate measures.

Couldn't the television condescend to demonstrate how to cook a potato? She had no desire to bake a pecan pie or attempt anything so grand as poaching a fish with sauce, as the strange, feminine little bearded man had prepared earlier on the television. She simply wanted a potato. A *cooked* potato.

After going to such lengths to disguise herself, hire a taxi, find a market, and (using her dwindling stash of bewildering American money) purchase the world's most uncookable potato and a few other food items, she had no stamina left to inquire as to how to prepare it.

How distressing to actually deal face-to-face with merchants, to be forced to count out currency, bill by bill. So very awkward, because American bills all looked the same. She seldom dealt with even her own nation's currency. And her

11

concept of "shopping" had never included anything remotely resembling a potato.

Once again she tried to spear the offending item with the evil fork, and could only wonder how one possibly fashioned french fries—crisp, delectable *pommes frites*—from a lumpy old potato. She did so love french fries, but such culinary marvels were quite beyond her skills. Logically enough, she imagined french fries must be fried in some way, but just how did one go about "frying"?

She was, of course, familiar with baked potatoes—lovely, fluffy baked potatoes topped with dabs of butter and chives. She could read English well enough to recognize the word "bake" on that stove knob-thing that also announced its connection with the "oven." Possibly the numbers on the knob advised of the various available temperatures in the oven. But Americans calibrated things so oddly.

After a quick review of the numbers, she chose 250 degrees as the desirable temperature for baking a potato. Two and one-half times 100 degrees Celsius, the point at which water boiled, should cook a potato quite nicely.

While the potato cooked, she might do well to practice her rudimentary domestic skills and retrieve the utensils she'd hurled in anger while unraveling the mysteries of cooking a potato.

Life hadn't prepared her to fend for herself, and she wondered if fleeing to this strange beach town so very far from home was the wisest decision.

But she had been betrayed—by her father, of all people! The man she'd trusted and relied on all her life. The humiliation of being forced to flee—to care for herself—*to travel without servants!*

This wide, flat beach bore not the least resemblance to her own beautiful, dazzling beach on the Mediterranean. This one was overrun with ill-behaved children, large ladies in one-piece bathing suits, and baggily attired adolescents in backwards caps, enraptured by thumping music. Not at all the sort of people with whom one would choose to mingle, even if one were inclined, or permitted, to do so.

Surely in this strange, unglamorous beach town, halfway down the southern peninsula of the United States, in the province—*pardon moi*, "state"—of Florida, no one would recognize her.

For the past few days, the tabloids had overflowed with pictures of her. But with her hair pulled back in a ponytail, and a floppy hat and cheap sunglasses firmly in place, she might never be recognized if no one looked closely.

Surely none of these provincials could possibly identify her as the scandalous fugitive the tabloids had christened "The Runaway Princess."

Princess Katriana of Île d'Arinedra.

Armed with his outrage at the clattering disturbance, and a fearsome need to tell somebody—anybody—off, Ian slammed his balled fist against the front door of the adjacent condo.

The lady who answered his knock was alarmingly beautiful, and armed with a lethal-looking fork. The voice growling swear words through the wall had been recognizably feminine, so it came as no surprise to find a woman at the door. But the luxurious mass of dark hair, the startling aquamarine eyes (at that moment spitting blue-green fire straight at him), the sculpted cheekbones, the full, almost pouty lips . . .

Ian was speechless. He was known as a glib interview around the racing circuit, always ready with a quip or a quote when somebody stuck a microphone in his face, no matter how bad his day had been, and of late his days had been bloody awful. But for those first few seconds, he could do little more than stare at the ethereal—and furious—vision in the doorway.

His first, reflexive thought was that she was the most exquisite woman he'd ever seen. After that, a brief surge of hormones reminded him exactly how long it had been since he'd physically enjoyed a woman like the one before him—or, indeed, any woman. By then, his good sense kicked in and demanded that he remove his head from his butt and to be wary of beautiful women. A bevy of young lovelies, or more exactly his pathetic weakness for them, had wrecked his marriage, which was why his beat-up body was alone in Daytona Beach while it attempted to heal.

"*Oui?*" the vision spat at him—in French, no less. The gorgeous lady with the fiery eyes and the quivering fork wasn't at all glad to see him.

And, by God, she had no idea who he was!

Everybody on earth, it seemed, knew Ian Grayson's face. He couldn't step into the men's room to take a leak without being asked for his autograph. Hard as hell to sign your name while trying to aim at a urinal.

"Is everything all right in here?" he asked. He tried to peer around the furious lady, while keeping an eye on her fork.

"Who are you?" There was an edge to her voice. Fear, perhaps?

"Ian Grayson," he answered. The famous smile, his trademark, which he threw in as a bonus, had no more effect on her than his name did.

"Why are you here?" she demanded.

"I live next door—well, not really *live*. I'm kind of staying next door—but I *do* own it—I—"

Shut up, Ian, he instructed firmly when he realized that he was babbling. *You sound like you're in junior high.*

"I'm from next door and I heard all the noise," he amended.

The beauty offered a fetching little shrug. "I was . . ." she searched for the proper word, ". . . upset."

Over her shoulder—for he was substantially taller than she—Ian spied various cooking pots, lids, utensils, baking sheets, and other pieces of kitchenware strewn across the living room, near the dividing wall they shared.

"Is there something I can do to help?" he asked. Indeed, he hoped there was *not* because this seemed to be some sort of a kitchen problem, and he was no great shakes in the kitchen. The vision in front of him appeared to be slightly psycho and her fork was aimed directly at his heart.

She considered his question, started to shake her head, then brightened. "Can you cook a potato?"

She spoke with an intriguing accent, drenched in equal parts naiveté and sensual energy. Her accent and cadence recalled his lusty boyhood passion for Sophia Loren. But wasn't Sophia Loren Italian? This exquisite little lady was unmistakably French.

But surely he had misunderstood. *Cook a potato?*

"A potato?" he repeated.

"*Oui.* I mean, yes, a potato. Can you cook a potato?"

"Cook it how?"

"Cook it done!"

"Cook it done," he repeated. No question about it, he was in the presence of a *lunatic.*

"So I can eat it. Not hard like a rock. Soft . . . like a . . . like a potato."

Ian considered the problem. The lady looked dead serious. "Yes, I can," he finally answered. He probably *could* cook a potato. He just couldn't remember ever actually doing it.

She smiled. Her eyes and a couple of enchanting dimples flashed, and Ian went weak. Not only did he distrust beautiful women, he also freely admitted to being afraid of them because beautiful women turned him into putty, a big glob of malleable goo with no willpower. He badly wanted to avoid this lovely, bizarre woman.

She smiled, inclined her head almost shyly, then murmured, "If you would be so kind."

Ian was hooked.

It seemed to be of the utmost importance to her that he cook a potato for her, and by God he was ready to cook twenty freakin' pounds of the things if that's what it took to make her happy.

She lowered the fork and stepped aside for him to enter the room.

The place was a wreck!

Most of the kitchen stuff lay haphazardly on one side of the living room floor, close to the wall. Numerous designer duds were strewn over the backs of chairs. A plate rested on the coffee table where she had been lounging while watching T.V. And on the carpet beside every seat in the room stood at least one unwashed glass.

And the kitchen was worse—much worse! Did she have a total disregard for housekeeping?

Ian's mother had spent all of his formative years pounding a sense of tidiness and order into him. He considered himself tolerant of many faults, but clutter wasn't one of them. This poor soul seemed to be at the opposite end of the spectrum—averse even to carrying her own dirty dishes back to the kitchen, let alone actually *washing* them.

He muttered something uncomplimentary.

His hostess, sensing his dismay, bristled and announced

16

stiffly, "Please excuse the disarray. The maids have not appeared."

"You have maids?"

"*Mais, oui*—but of course." She looked very confident at first. Then he watched all that confidence drain away. "Surely there are maids," she finished with visible desperation. She swiped a hand through her glorious mass of hair, pulling it back off her face, and surveyed the mess she'd made.

"You don't know if you have maids or not?"

"This is not exactly my—my home."

Ian considered suggesting that if this place weren't her home, she might consider taking better care of it. But that was *her* problem. He had his own problems—his own *huge* problems—and no energy or inclination to take on anyone else's. This place needed some serious work, and he itched to roll up his sleeves, plunge in and start cleaning up the clutter. Only two reasons held him back: he didn't want this woman to think him strange, and, of course, his pride. His career might currently be bobbing around in the toilet, but, by God, he hadn't sunk to being a houseboy. Not yet, anyway.

"Where exactly *is* your home?" His question was more curious than polite, and it sounded that way.

The woman waved her fork in the air like a magic wand. "Oh, over . . . over there someplace," she replied.

He let his curious gaze try to follow the trajectory of the twirling fork. He realized that he was peering into the dining area, out the sliding glass doors onto the patio, then ultimately toward the ocean.

Toward Europe, perhaps?

"So what are you doing here?"

Her hand—the one holding the fork—once more claimed his attention. It no longer twirled in the general direction of

17

Europe. It angled sharply toward his crotch.

"Hey, no harm meant," he tried to assure her, then prudently stepped out of her reach. If the lady went bonkers and started poking that damn fork into him, he preferred to confine the damage to someplace other than where the fork was pointed. That happened to be one of the few body parts still working reasonably well, and he didn't need a fork stuck in it.

"Will you help me?" she asked.

Ian shot an inquiring look back at her. Her voice had grown thin and pitiful, and he realized that her question encompassed much more than cooking a potato. Her air of arrogance crumbled. What he saw before him now was fear in its simplest form.

He wanted to say *no*. He disliked his own selfish streak but couldn't afford to involve himself with this woman and her problems. The sheer force of her beauty demanded that he avoid her like the plague. Of course, that hard-and-fast rule was written with some fine print that allowed him to sometimes spend a night or two with a beautiful woman. But no emotional involvement allowed. None. And this lady obviously came with some major baggage, perhaps even a touch of insanity—and the definite need for a maid.

Why did she look familiar?

Something about the eyes. That hair. The haughty tilt of the head. Her elegant neck. He had seen her before, and not long ago. But where?

Much of the last several months had passed in a haze as he lay in the hospital. Aside from that, he had been no other place than the liquor store, the grocery store, the beach (site of his daily attempts at jogging), and on his couch, plopped in front of the TV.

"Who are you?" he asked. As the words left his mouth he realized that he'd asked the wrong question. *What is your name?* Or maybe *Have we met?* would have been more proper, less suspicious.

"Mon dieu!" Her lips formed the words silently. Ian was no master of reading lips, most particularly French ones, but he recognized the words. He watched the color drain from the woman's face and the tears rise and pool in her eyes.

That's when he realized who she was.

From the television. And from the supermarket tabloids, which he despised but out of sheer boredom now bought and read from cover to cover. Her picture was everywhere, but he had missed the clues: the fabulous mane of hair, French accent, and her inability to perform the simplest tasks on her own. Missing were the huge Jackie Kennedy sunglasses she customarily sported, but everything else about this woman betrayed her identity.

Fate was playing tricks on him again. Because Ian Grayson, washed-up, broken-down race-car driver—a man fixated on his past because he had no discernable future—had stumbled straight into the middle of the biggest story to hit the news since O.J.'s glove hadn't fit.

Somehow he had managed to find the Runaway Princess.

He was a scary man, tall, lanky, grim-faced and evidently disinclined to shave. His chocolate-brown eyes, thickly ringed with lashes that she would have killed to possess, were too inquisitive. They gave him away the instant he realized her identity.

Who are you? he had asked. His eyes informed her that he had realized the answer.

"If I tell you then I must kill you," she shot back in a wretched attempt at American humor. She didn't pull off either the humor or the accent particularly well.

Or maybe she did.

The man threw his head back and laughed, but his laughter had a strange, bitter undertone.

And, *mon dieu,* what earth-shattering dimples he had! Far more appealing than her own outstanding dimples. There was also a surprising kindness in his eyes, almost a sense of sympathy.

"That, darlin', might just be the high point of my day," he said. Very strange words, indeed.

"Killing you?"

"Lady, I'd be willing to bet you don't have any idea how to properly stomp a bug, much less kill an old coot like me. What did you plan to do? Run me through with that fork?"

She racked her brain for some French equivalent of "old coot." Could it be some reference to overcooked food?

"Besides that, Princess," he shot her another of those wicked smiles he so generously doled out, "if you kill me, who's gonna cook your potato?"

Despite the challenge in his words, his smile was reassuring—and a little exciting, if she allowed herself to face that truth. It made her heart race, her breath catch . . . caused heat to rise to her face. She wanted to fear this man. After all, he had unearthed her secret. She dared not speculate on what he might do with that knowledge. But how could one fear a laughing man with dimples? Even though the way he rolled the word *Princess* around in his mouth was almost depraved.

"You can be trusted, I assume?" she asked warily.

"First off, Princess," he growled, "never assume anything, *ever.* Second, no, I can't be trusted. Third—ahhhh, geez—now don't start crying—please."

It was too late.

The tears rolled down her face, complete with dreadfully unpleasant nose snorts. The whole episode was unfortunate in the extreme.

She was crying! *Actually crying*—violating the most rudimentary of standards. A princess might show her displeasure in any number of proscribed ways, but she had broken the fundamental and most basic rule of conduct.

A princess *never* cried.

Jesus H. Christ! How does a guy get himself into a mess like this? Ian wondered. There he stood, clumsily trying to comfort a fruitcake princess who had run away from daddy, if his memory of the tabloid stories was correct, for some obscure reason. He patted her shoulder awkwardly.

Then his disobedient arms reached out, of their own sudden volition, and folded around her. He had no more control over their actions than he had over the rising and setting of the sun. All he could think to do was hold her and let her cry.

"You are very kind," she murmured into his shoulder.

"Not particularly," he answered. He wanted no credit for anything. He especially didn't want this woman looking to him for comfort. All he wanted was *out of here!*

"I'm not usually this emotional, you know."

"No, I didn't know."

Eventually, she composed herself and stepped away from him. Ian was thankful for that because his body had decided that it liked this princess-on-the-lam. It liked her *a lot.* And even though his brain kept shouting that it wanted nothing to do with her, his body was proceeding through its routine checklist and readying the equipment for blastoff.

He was sure she was still holding that fork.

"I do apologize," she said.

"Accepted."

An uncomfortable silence hung between them.

"What were you saying about a potato?" Ian offered as an

alternative to the silence. It was either that or clear his throat. Surely to heaven, in his few weeks of isolation his social skills hadn't regressed to throat-clearing.

"Oh, would you? Would you, please?"

"I might be persuaded. But don't let that give you the impression that I'm easy, 'cause I'm not." He punctuated it with a wink.

She looked at him strangely. It was obvious that she had no idea what he was talking about.

"Forget it," he sighed.

They moved toward the kitchen, picking their way through the minefield of glasses, clothes, newspapers and kitchen items littering the floor. "Maybe we should pick up some of this stuff," Ian suggested. "I doubt that a maid is gonna show up here anytime soon." He thought himself quite clever to throw in the *we*. Surely she would take the hint that *we* really meant *you*.

"Oh, would you? I would appreciate it very much."

So much for clever hints. Quite obviously, Mediterranean royalty didn't pick up on those very quickly.

Except maybe the assortment of movie stars and dancey-boy-band singers who frequently vacationed in luxury in her island kingdom just over the horizon from the South of France. At least that's the tale the tabloids told. Normally he didn't put much stock in gossip, but now having met her, he could easily envision the lovely princess and her pack of celebrity studs frolicking naked in daddy's marble pool or toasting the polo ponies from the royal yacht or whatever-the-hell-else people like that did when they got together and weren't banging the hell out of each other.

"My potato is in the oven. There," Katriana announced. She pointed with pride toward the oven as if she had just invented it.

"So what's the problem?" Ian asked. With her potato baking away happily in the oven, she seemed to have more or less figured out the cooking process.

"I'm not sure."

He stepped over a sack of groceries sitting on the floor. Probably the bag had never made it to the counter because there was no more room for it there. Plates, glasses and silverware lay there in their unwashed splendor.

"Well, why don't we take a look?" Ian suggested. This was almost like dealing with a child—or a Martian.

One glance at the oven temperature, and a quick check of the cold potato in the barely warm oven confirmed that her cooking skills were on a par with her housekeeping skills. *Subpar.*

"Well, now, there you go. That's your problem. Look here, Princess." He set the oven temperature higher—much, much higher. "The way it was set, you might have your potato cooked by sometime next week. This ought to help."

"Will it be long?"

"Maybe an hour. That's quite a potato you've got in there."

"*An hour?*" Princess Katriana was *not* happy.

"Listen, Princess, that's the best I can do. Now, look at the clock and in an hour go turn that knob to *Off* and take your potato out and eat it. You *can* tell time, can't you?" he finished with a nasty little smirk. He couldn't help himself. And since he was on a roll, he added, "While it's cooking, you might want to tidy this place up a little."

"*Excusez-moi?*" The royal back went ramrod straight. The royal eyebrow inched upward. Ian discovered that the royal gaze could cut like a knife.

"You—might—want—to—tidy—up—a—little," he repeated, slow and loud, as if that might enable her to understand. Although he was afraid it wasn't the words that she didn't understand, it was the concept of *tidying*.

She looked distressed, then changed the subject. "Can you open a tin of food?"

Ian couldn't believe it. In fact, he had a burning need to throw his hands up in the air and howl with frustration, to bite something, to cuss and spit and growl like a dog. "Open a tin of food? Did you say *open a tin of food?*"

"*Oui.* I have these tins of food, but I cannot get into them. How does one do that?" she wondered, head cocked to one side, genuinely curious.

Ian found her annoying as hell, yet at the same time bewitching. Her actions and her accent were so . . . so *French* . . . for lack of a better word. And so guileless, it could almost bring tears to a guy's eyes.

She was far from home and out of her element. She couldn't survive forever on baked potatoes, so it looked like he would have to feed her, or at least teach her how to cook—which ought to be damned interesting because he couldn't cook either. The poor lady didn't know how to use a can opener, or even realize that such a device existed.

For sure, he was going to have to clean up her mess or she might disappear into the clutter and never be found again. He vowed to do so only once, however. He *did* have his limits.

This woman was a royal pain in the ass.

He stopped grousing and smiled. Yes, that's exactly what she was. A *royal* pain in the ass.

Chapter 2

Ian Grayson, the man from next door, swore that he was not a chef by trade, but he prepared and served a delightful dinner. For all the trouble that wretched potato had given her earlier, it behaved impeccably for him. He supplied salt, pepper, butter, cheese, even sour cream from his own quarters next door, along with a lumpy, oddly shaped, American delicacy called a "frozen burrito," which he popped into the oven to cook alongside the potato. It resembled a crepe, yet was filled with something meaty and spicy, Spanish in flavor. She loved it.

And she told him so.

"Well, hell, I couldn't let you starve," he answered curtly. Possibly Monsieur Grayson was too busy to make conversation just then because he was energetically "tidying up." His term, not hers.

"You know what?" he wondered during one intense flurry of tidying.

"What?"

"If you'd use one item at a time and put it away, you wouldn't end up with a mess like this."

Katriana chose to ignore that rude remark. The condition of her quarters was embarrassing, but she had expected a brigade of maids—or at the very least, one maid—to eventually appear and attend to the clutter.

How did one survive without servants?

She pondered her new life and its absence of menial staff

until he called to her again, this time from the kitchen.

"Well, you cleaned your plate just fine, didn't you, Princess?"

How unkind, and uncouth, of the man to draw attention to such behavior! Katriana was quite aware that proper decorum demanded nibbling at one's food and, of course, one must never, never gulp it down, but she had never before been so hungry.

In any event, Monsieur Grayson possessed his own set of shortcomings. By far his greatest defect, other than his delight in drawing attention to her untidy habits—and his eternal penchant for "tidying up"—was that he had served dinner without wine. Clearly, wine with dinner was not a necessity to men of his particular class. In truth, it would have been difficult for Katriana herself to select the proper wine to accompany the frozen burrito, so perhaps that was why no wine had been served.

But the chilled beer he had provided to accompany her dinner would have been her last choice. In the end, however, it was enjoyable. Americans were so strange about chilling their beverages with ice. She had expected the man to dump cubes of ice directly into her beer. *Mais non.* He merely plopped the frosty beer down in front of her and instructed her to drink it straight from the bottle. The experience was rather like she imagined camping might be.

Chilled beer also had an alarming tendency to make one want to giggle for no reason at all. Until . . .

"Now, bring your dishes on in here," he called from the kitchen, "and we're gonna have a lesson in something I bet you've never done before in your life."

Katriana shot him a glare. There was kindness in this man, but he also had a nasty mean streak.

"I have no doubt," she muttered. But she more or less graciously—in truth, probably *less*—picked up her plate and silverware, even the empty beer bottle, and carried them to him in the kitchen.

"OK, Princess, meet the dishwasher."

"Why?"

"Because that's where your dirty dishes go."

"I am aware of the dishwasher."

"But are you aware that the dishes don't jump into it by themselves?"

At that moment, Katriana decided that Ian Grayson, for all of his earlier kindness, was detestable.

"This is how you do it," he continued and threw in a brief demonstration, as if his lecture itself weren't annoying enough. "A little rinse with the hot water, then down in the racks like this."

To Katriana's chagrin, it was a simple process, even when she herself did it. And he made sure that she actually did most of it herself.

"It's no big deal if you do this every time you have a dirty—excuse me, I suppose princesses don't *dirty* their dishes—every time you *use* a dish."

"There is no need to be sarcastic, Monsieur Grayson. I grasp the concept."

"Do you grasp the concept enough to be able to do it yourself next time?"

"I suspect that I can manage."

"Do you understand now that there are no maids? That there will be no maids?"

"*Oui,*" she growled through clenched teeth.

She watched him work diligently to cultivate an air of sincerity and earnestness, but she suspected that there wasn't an ounce of sincerity or earnestness to be found in his body. He was a cretin, an ill-behaved, bossy beast of a man, who

27

seemed to take particular delight in her unfortunate circumstances. Just because he had saved her from starvation gave him no right to school her on the niceties of housekeeping. She too enjoyed pristine quarters, but there were times when it was not possible. This was one of those times.

"Do you understand that *I'm* not the maid?"

"*Oui,* Monsieur Grayson. However, you must understand that I am unaccustomed—" she began to explain, but he refused her even the small courtesy of allowing her to continue.

"Princess, I am unaccustomed also," he barked back. "I'm not an amicable village idiot who wanders around blissfully doing other people's chores. I'm a celebrity myself over here on this side of the pond. I have *a lot* of money. I have maids of my own. And I can assure you that when I'm at home I certainly don't do cleaning for myself. I'm too busy. I don't have the time. But if I have to, I can. Like now."

"So I see."

Ian Grayson didn't appear busy, or rich, to her. When he had knocked on her door, he'd had the look of someone who had just woken from a nap. How busy or rich could the man be if he slept in the afternoon?

"And so can you."

"I am not your child, Monsieur Grayson," Katriana declared. "I am not your responsibility." Somewhere inside the man beat a kind heart, and he had indeed assisted her, but all that kindness was overshadowed by his need to reproach. Perhaps it was time for her to again act like a princess instead of a child waiting patiently for her next reprimand.

"I shall make every attempt to pick up my things," she enunciated, holding her head at its full, regal tilt. This discussion brought to mind a recent ill-fated confrontation with her father that had led directly to her current desperate straits.

But at the moment she was focused on Ian Grayson and his unfortunate propensity for instilling in her the one trait that a succession of nannies, governesses, and tutors had neglected: the virtue of neatness.

"I shall run hot water over every dish and glass that I use, then place them inside the dishwasher. If a celebrity like yourself can perform these duties, then I have no doubt that with a bit of practice, I too can become proficient. I really am quite clever, in spite of what you think of me."

He must have found humor in that remark, because his mouth creased into a smile. A charming smile. A devastating smile that left her knees weak and her heart fluttering. Katriana found that smile confusing—almost alarming. Those dimples should be registered as lethal weapons. His smile transformed him from the grouchy curmudgeon fixated on "tidying up" into . . . into something else entirely. Something Katriana was unable to define.

She wished he would leave. Her life was in enough disarray without the complications he brought to it.

"Are we through now?" she asked—still at her regal best.

"Not even close," he answered, his grin still firmly in place. In spite of his kindness, she wanted to hate him and his pushy ways, but that wasn't quite possible . . .

. . . until he hinted at what their next adventure would be.

"So, Princess, you want to tell me what you know about scrubbing a bathroom?"

An hour later, Ian had begun to doubt his own sanity. Had he lain dormant in the hospital too long? Gone mushy? He must have suffered a far more serious head injury than his doctors had diagnosed. If he wasn't insane, then the boredom of the last few months was taking a strange and appalling toll.

Why else would he appoint himself chief cook and housecleaner for Île d'Arinedra's most famous fugitive? He didn't know squat about royalty, except that this one was a messy little thing. And she liked burritos with beer.

He caught himself smiling. Princess Katriana's digestion was every bit as commendable as her lineage.

"Don't you think it's about time you told me what's going on?" he asked her, not expecting a straight answer. He was simply making noise because he hated silence. He was accustomed to roaring engines, pushy fans, inquisitive reporters. Everything in his life made noise. Silence and inactivity were unfamiliar factors, and for much too long now they had also been his closest companions.

His brief flurry of domesticity had relieved the inactivity, but now his bad leg ached like a son-of-a—something. He eased it up and stretched it out lengthwise on the couch, sneaker and all. The princess was installed regally in a side chair, her back ramrod-straight, her feet angled to the left and crossed just so at the ankles, exactly as she had been taught in finishing school.

"I ran away. That's what happened," she replied in her best *up yours* princess voice.

"Lady, I know you ran away. Every person in the free world with access to a newspaper knows you ran away. I want to know why. And how."

"It's a bit personal," she declared, nose elevated just the barest bit, as if it had caught a whiff of some foul odor. Ian gave the lady credit. She seemed quite capable of out-snobbing anybody, anywhere, anytime, if the mood overtook her. But sometimes, when she wasn't concentrating, when she let down her guard . . .

Get over it, buddy, he told himself. He didn't much care for the way her smile—the few times she had deigned to smile—

warmed his middle. Or the way his heart pattered (like that of a teenager in hormonal meltdown) when she floated past and he caught a whiff of her perfume. Or the fierce way his body had reacted while she cried in his arms. Too much time without a woman could have embarrassing, awful consequences.

It could also make him do stupid stuff—like houseclean. Like gather up the royal dainties from the floor and run 'em through the washer, in spite of Her Majesty's raving about the care of fine silk. But he drew the line at hand washing the lady's underwear. If those exquisite wisps of lace ended up in shreds, then that was just too damned bad! He was a racecar driver, not the laundry boy. He was crazy as hell to be doing any of this in the first place.

But that unwanted heat seared away at his insides. Played with his senses, rolled around inside him. He couldn't even blame it on the burrito. Princess Nose-in-the-Air over there, perched on her chair like the Queen of England, had consumed his one and only burrito, wolfed it down like she was starving, but always with her knife and fork held at the correct angle.

"God knows I don't care anything about your deep, dark secrets," Ian informed her, "but somehow I ended up in the middle of this situation, and I think I ought to have some idea what I've gotten myself into. Don't you?"

"Perhaps," she replied, to all appearances quite bored.

"Lady, you're copping an attitude with the wrong guy. It may have slipped your royal mind, but I'm on *your* side. Hell, I even fed you my last burrito."

Katriana brightened. "And it was lovely," she trilled and turned on her electric smile, etched with those two enchanting dimples that made him want to drool and trace each one with his tongue. He direly needed to work up some resistance to this woman if she was going to be around for very long. All this churning, this unwanted, embarrassing, uncontrollable *rigidity* wasn't good for his healing process. And it made him cranky.

Just in case his various parts weren't behaving as well as they should, he turned himself around and lowered the painful, overused leg back to the floor. He was thinking impure thoughts and probably shouldn't be sitting with his legs splayed apart.

"It is *très difficile* to explain, but I shall try," Katriana murmured. She looked distressed.

Ian felt like a villain as he watched her search for words. Her English was adequate, but she had a tendency to pepper it with French. The more upset she grew, the more French he had to translate.

"Why don't you just hit the high points?" he suggested. "We'll fill in the blanks later if we have to."

Katriana smiled—and heat assaulted every part of him again. Primitive heat skittered through his veins and pooled dangerously low. He realized he must be grinning like a half-wit at her, but he couldn't do much about it. She was baring her soul to him and he wasn't able to pay attention to a word of it. Until . . .

". . . and please don't think me *grossière*—rude—but I am only twenty-three years and have no wish to be married to a man who is seventy-nine-years-old. Perhaps if I knew him or even—"

"What did you just say?" *Surely he hadn't heard that right!*

"Perhaps if I knew him—"

"Knew who?"

"Sir Christian Walcott, of England. The man I was—am—betrothed to marry."

"And he's—what did you say?—*seventy-nine years old?*"

"*Oui.*"

Ian shook his head to clear away the heat-induced fog. While he was sailing around in la-la land, Katriana had dropped a bomb, and he had missed its revelation. "So that's why you ran away?"

"*Oui.* It was the action of a child, but the chance arose and I took it."

"One quick question. How did the opportunity arise? For someone as visible as you to disappear, it must take incredible planning."

"It was *très facile. En vérité,* it was not even my idea, but I was overjoyed when the possibility was presented to me."

"So tell me, who presented that possibility to you?" Good God in heaven! He was beginning to imitate her speech. Quite a departure for a guy who perpetually watched his own language to keep from peppering it with liberal doses of *ain't.*

"*Soeur* Marie Giselle."

"Who the hell is Sewer Marie Giselle? What kind of a name is that?"

"*Soeur* Marie Giselle is one of the teaching nuns charged with my education."

"Oh—" He caught himself just in time to keep from adding the word *shit* to his statement. He knew nothing at all of teaching nuns, but he did know enough not to say *shit* when discussing them.

His *oh* must have been a satisfactory response, because Katriana continued on with her story.

"Soeur Marie Giselle told me that if I married Sir Christian, the marriage would not be pleasing in the eyes of God. Because of his age, Sir Christian would be incapable of fathering a child, and such a relationship without the possibility of a child is a sin. She also said it was an abomination for me to waste myself on a man of his advanced years."

Ian thought he might be blushing. He hoped not, but the

33

heat rushing to his face was a good indication that he was. Now he regretted questioning the logistics of her escape.

"Soeur Marie Giselle has family members in this country and she took it upon herself to make the necessary arrangements for money and lodging for me here," Katriana continued. "A trip was already planned for me to New York to add bits and pieces to my trousseau. Once I was in New York, the plan was, as I said, *très facile* to carry out. A courier simply delivered to me an envelope marked *confidentiel,* which contained American currency, an airplane ticket, an address and a key to this place, which belongs, I believe, to Soeur Marie Giselle's brother and his family. It is quite fortunate that they do not live here the entire year, but merely use it as a vacation home. When the moment arose that no one was watching me, I walked out the door and left."

Ian had to call time-out to consider her strange story. "Excuse me, but I don't understand why are you supposed to marry this old guy."

"Sir Christian was a mentor to my father, and my father owes a debt to him," Katriana explained. She paused; then, with a hint of tears from those unbelievable eyes, summed up her dilemma: "I am to be the payment."

"Let me get this straight. Your daddy, the King of—

"Île d'Arinedra is a principality. We have no king. My father is a prince, as is my brother. Jean-Luc, of course, will reign upon my father's death. I am merely the second child, and a daughter, so I shall never reign. I am little better than a commoner."

"So Daddy's trying to marry you off to pay a debt?"

"You must understand that it is a debt of honor. If it were a monetary debt, I doubt that I would be in such circumstances. My father's honor is at stake, not his fortune. These two are very different, you see."

"No, I *don't* see," Ian declared. "I don't see how your father can hand you over to some old man so he can play with you, no matter what the old guy did for him. That's archaic. It's unnatural."

Katriana laughed—slightly. It sounded stilted and forced. "Not for my father."

"Well, I can't let that happen."

Who the hell said that? Ian wondered, shocked. It sounded like him. But why? He had no reason to become involved in this fight. Too bad about the beautiful princess being forced to marry the old codger, but how much help could he be? And why should he even care?

"Monsieur Grayson, you are very kind, but I do not see what you could possibly do about it," she told him. "I do not even see what I can do about it."

"Lady, you've managed this far. Don't give up now and waste all that effort. I'm not exactly Rambo, but I'll do what I can to help you," he offered.

His brain must be damaged far worse than the doctors had originally thought.

"*Merci,* Monsieur Graham," she murmured and inclined her head graciously. Ian was afraid he might cry. This fairy-tale princess was teetering on the edge of disaster. Almost overnight, she'd become one of the most recognizable women in the world. She was adrift in a strange country yet incapable of caring for herself in the simplest way. "I cannot stay here forever, of course," she continued, "but I am waiting for inspiration, for a miracle to present itself."

"Better not pin your hopes on a miracle, Princess. It almost never happens that way."

"I realize. But truly, Monsieur Grayson, do you have a better idea?"

"No," he muttered, trying to bat away the preposterous

idea taking root in his head. He couldn't recall ever having such hideous delusions as the one he was experiencing now, not even in his drinking days.

"I will wait here for a few more days, then I must either have a plan or I must return home in disgrace and honor my father's wishes."

"What kind of plan?"

"Well . . . ," she started to explain, then stopped, confused. "I'm not sure." English translations didn't seem to pose as great a problem for her as her uncertain future did. "I am afraid I have made *une erreur infortune*. I should not have come here."

"Lady, I gotta agree you're in a big mess right now, but I'll help you if I can."

"How could you possibly ensure that I will never have to marry that old man, who is older than my grandfather?" Katriana demanded. The cool and regal princess was nowhere to be found. In her place stood an irate, almost desperate woman with a huge problem.

His unwelcome ghost of an idea swirled around, struggling to take shape. None of the specifics were yet clear, but the bare essence of the idea scared him witless. Because the only way Ian's poor, lust-clouded, not-quite-healed-yet-from-the-wreck brain could see to help the lady out of her current predicament was to marry her.

The other voice in his psyche, the intelligent one, insisted that such an idea was beyond ludicrous. The very last step he wanted to take was to get married again, whatever the circumstances. Once was one time too many.

No. Actually, marriage was the second-to-last thing he wanted. Caring for a damned snotty, prima donna princess was the *last* thing.

But Katriana was so vulnerable and lost and unprepared

to live on her own. Her status in life demanded that she be pampered and cared for, not forced to hide out alone like a criminal. Marriage was extreme, but he saw no better way. He was unattached, and would make sure to get unattached again at the first possible opportunity; but in the interim, marriage to him would keep her legally in the United States and out of her father's control.

He also knew he had a darker, more selfish reason. A few months ago he had faced his own mortality, alone. The experience had terrified him. He especially didn't like to think that if he'd died from his injuries, no one would have missed him. Drivers were replaced with ridiculous ease. But quick and easy substitutes for trusted companions were not so easily found. He would not *really* be a husband to poor, desperate—but so very beautiful—Princess Katriana. She'd not be inclined to share her delectable body with the likes of him. But they could share a bit of companionship, maybe even friendship and trust. If he wrecked again, crashed into another wall and never woke up, there would be at least one person with a bit of a reason to miss him. One lone person, who could speak up and declare that selfish, hedonistic Ian Grayson had once done a kind, honorable deed.

"I have no idea how I can help," he lied as he tried to file away the world's dumbest idea under the heading of "very last resort". "But I haven't given up, and don't you give up either."

"Why should you care about what happens to me, Monsieur Grayson?" Katriana asked.

"Damned if I know," Ian replied, meaning every word of it. "Damned if I know."

Chapter 3

Katriana's father's henchmen were already closing in.

Ian realized that when one of them—a *big* one—stopped him before dawn the next morning. It happened while he was in the process of hobbling back up the steps from the beach after his morning run, just as the sky began to lighten.

He made an effort to run every morning, always before sunrise. His injured leg still wasn't fit, and he jogged like a gimpy old man. God help him if any fan saw how he ran, because word would soon spread that Ian Grayson's career was over. If nobody knew for sure, there was still a ray of hope that he might be able to one day continue doing the only thing he knew how to do: race.

" 'Scuse me, buddy," said a big hulk of a guy in a suit, materializing out of the half-light of dawn. His words were a mere formality. A fleet of bulldozers couldn't fight their way past a man of that size, and most certainly not one worn-out guy with a leg that sometimes worked and sometimes didn't.

Ian grunted his response. He didn't like the looks of the guy or his suit. Nobody wore a suit at the beach in late August.

"Have you seen this girl?" The big guy thrust his meaty fist up in front of Ian's nose. From the glow of the security light near the steps, Ian saw gripped in that fist a photograph of Katriana.

"That's what's-her-name, isn't it?" Ian responded, not

answering the question. *Who the hell was this guy, anyway?*

"Yeah."

Ian hoped like hell that the guy in the suit didn't notice how he was manipulating the conversation, evading the specific question asked of him.

"I didn't ask who she was. I asked if you'd seen her," the thug pointed out. Evidently he was brighter than he looked. And just as clearly Ian's scheme was nowhere near as clever as he'd thought.

"Seen her where?"

"Seen her here, buddy."

"Here?" Ian inquired, looking around, eyebrows raised in feigned disbelief.

"Anywhere. You seen her anywhere?"

Ian's gaze returned to the picture of Katriana. She was strolling along a ritzy Mediterranean beach, her magnificent hair flying in the wind, her bikini revealing some memorable curves. "Nah."

"You sure?"

"I'd remember *that* if I ever saw it." He nudged the guy. "Wouldn't you?"

"Spoiled brat," the guy spat back. "Some crazy European princess. I don't know why her daddy wants her back, but he does."

Ian laughed. Then, with as much nonchalance as he could muster—given his racing heart, his inability to draw a decent breath, and his sudden awareness that this man probably carried a gun, he asked, "Why are you questioning me? Has she been spotted around here?"

"Some local thought he saw her yesterday in the grocery store."

Ian nudged the guy again and pooh-poohed with polite disbelief, "In the *grocery store?*"

"Yeah. Go figure that one out."

"Sounds like your tipster might be on drugs," Ian suggested. The guy made an effort to smile, but wasn't very successful.

"Could be. Not many druggies hang around grocery stores, though."

"Not many princesses do either," Ian countered.

"Yeah, well—" The goon tugged at his tie. The rising sun was bringing the Florida heat with it. "That too."

Ian considered his next move carefully, aware that he must cultivate just the right tone, a fine balance of curiosity and disinterest. Being James Bond wasn't as easy as it looked in the movies.

"What are you supposed to do with her if you find her?"

"You're kind of a nosy fellow, aren't you?" the guy noted. He peered at Ian, tugged at his tie again, then squinted and peered at Ian some more.

"Not especially. Just being polite."

The thug flashed a genuine grin at him. "You're that racer guy, aren't you?"

"I'm *a* racer guy. I'm not sure if I'm *that* racer guy," Ian sparred back. "Which racer guy are you talking about?"

"Oh, you're him, all right. The one in that bad wreck at the speedway back in February. I watched it on TV. I thought you were dead."

Ian pasted on his famous smile, the one that drove women crazy. He doubted that it had quite the same effect on the guy in the suit, but he threw all his charm into it. To Ian's dismay, his smile felt forced—strange and unfamiliar. But he forged ahead anyway. "Well, that makes two of us. I thought I was dead, too."

The guy relaxed a little. He was still smiling.

"Say," Ian continued, "have you got a card with your

phone number on it?"

"Sure."

"Let me have it. I'm up and down the beach a lot. I'll watch for her and call you if I see her."

"Well that's real nice of you, buddy."

"No problem."

He reached in his pocket and produced a card. His name was Basil Burke and—*holy shit!*—Basil Burke was a Pinkerton detective!

Poor Princess Katriana's goose was as good as cooked. Evading a Pinkerton detective was no task for the faint of heart. And despite her flashes of spunk, Katriana seemed to be blessed with a faint heart.

"Say, buddy—Ian." For the first time, the detective sounded almost shy—starstruck, perhaps. Ian could only hope. "Could I have your autograph?"

"Sure thing, Basil," Ian answered and tried flashing his world-famous smile again, glad that he'd noted the name on the card. "You got something to write on? I seem to be fresh out." He pretended to pat himself down for a pen and paper. Not much chance of finding one, since he was wearing running shorts and a tee shirt.

"Here." Basil presented another of his business cards, blank side up. He shuffled from one foot to the other while Ian wrote a glowing personal note to Basil from his new, good friend Ian Grayson. Ian added his autograph with his usual flourish.

"There you go," Ian said as he handed back the card. "Look me up if you get to a race." He chucked Basil on one of his substantial shoulders. "Maybe we can have a beer or you can hang around in the pits or something."

Ian neglected to mention that there were no races scheduled in his future. Even if there were, how could he possibly crawl in and out of the car through the window, with a gimpy leg and a back that didn't respond very well when asked to bend? There was also the little problem with his brain that the doctors had warned him about. It would cease functioning altogether if he dared to knock it against a concrete wall again. But Basil didn't need to know these facts. Nobody needed to know them except Ian.

Basil beamed.

Ian shook his hand, chucked Basil's shoulder one more time and vowed, "I'll keep my eye out for what's-her-name. She'll be hard to miss if she's around here anyplace, 'specially if she's wearing that bathing suit." Then they shared a chuckle—two men of the world who knew the score.

They parted ways, and Ian watched as Basil loped down the concrete steps to the beach then turned north. He was relieved that he had a skeleton Plan B in place, because Princess Katriana's Plan A had just gone up in smoke. Plan B was ridiculous and didn't have a chance in hell of working, but at the moment it was the only chance she had.

Katriana munched on her Pop-Tart. Quite a tasty little thing, she decided. The dollop of jam in the middle could be less gummy and the pastry wasn't as flaky as she was accustomed to, but she could overlook those minor shortcomings—*because Pop-Tarts required no cooking!* How long, she wondered, could a person live on nothing but Pop-Tarts?

Contemplating Pop-Tarts was much more pleasant than contemplating her circumstances, which were becoming grim. She should be doing something—something positive, something brave and bold—anything at all to prolong her freedom.

Everything about this new life was frightening—including the sudden brisk knock on the front door. She froze, silent and motionless until Monsieur Grayson growled at her through the door, low and throaty, "It's me. Ian. Let me in."

Relieved, she exhaled and rose to open the door.

"*Bonjour,*" she greeted him, smiling wide and striving to sound pleasant and polite. Such courtesies had been drummed mercilessly into her by the teaching nuns as well as her father.

"Princess, the *jour*'s not too damned *bon* right now, and it's not even seven o'clock yet."

Monsieur Grayson seemed to be in a foul mood. He was also sweaty and unkempt, both abominable traits in a man. But, *mon dieu,* he filled out those running shorts magnificently.

There was too much of the man. He was too intense. Too dark and dangerous, too bossy, too fastidious. His dimples were too appealing. Katriana tried to focus her attention on those wonderful dimples.

"Is there a problem?" she asked.

"That depends on how serious you are about staying hidden from daddy and his number one choice for a son-in-law."

"I beg your pardon?"

"Pay attention, Princess," he ordered. "This is important. There's a Pinkerton detective outside cruising the beach looking for you, right now."

"What is a Pinkerton detective?"

Ian ran a hand through his sweaty cap of curls. He was so irritated and upset that his distress was almost tangible. "Do you have any idea what a detective is?"

"*Oui.* A man who finds people, or follows people, perhaps."

"Bingo," he answered and pointed his finger at her like a gun. "And this one has followed you and found you. He

43

works for a company called Pinkerton. And lady, Pinkerton has been around for more than a century because they *always* find their man. Always."

"Monsieur Grayson—"

"Call me Ian, Princess," he interrupted, looking stern, almost fearsome. "You're going to have to call me Ian."

"Ian," she repeated dutifully, expecting the word to feel strange and awkward on her tongue. It didn't. It flowed. It tingled. It filled her mouth like warm honey. She much preferred to call him Monsieur Grayson.

Ian's face softened. Its severity melted away, replaced by a potent dose of dimples and a thoroughly bewitching smile. Katriana forgot to breathe. She forgot what she was saying. She forgot everything.

Perhaps, her behavior could be attributed to her upbringing. Perhaps other women were not this uncomfortable alone in a man's presence, even such a magnificent man as Ian Grayson. But Katriana had never before been alone, unchaperoned, with any man. Not even with her brother. Surely that was why she found her reaction to Ian so unsettling. He was indeed a bossy man, much like her father, but without her father's selfish arrogance.

Her instincts told her to trust him, but had he not warned her that he was not to be trusted? Was he in fact untrustworthy, or had he lied? Neither scenario appealed to her. Yet he seemed to care about her circumstances. And without him, she was very alone.

"Ian," she repeated, and again she tingled when she said his name. She tried to ignore the sensation. "In spite of what I said last night, I cannot go back. I simply cannot. Not only will I be punished, but I assure you, despite any protest I might make—and in light of what I have done to embarrass my father, as well as Sir Christian—the wedding plans will proceed rapidly. My father has promised me to this man. He has given his word, and there is no doubt that I will be forced to consummate the transaction."

"What about your mother?" Ian asked. "Doesn't your mother have anything to say about this?"

"My mother died when I was five. I remember very little about her. I remember kindness and warm arms and soft kisses when I went to bed. And she smelled wonderful." Why was it important that Ian understand that someone had once loved her? "I can still smell her—like powder and roses."

Ian peered down at her and Katriana could see sympathy in his chocolate-brown eyes. "Of course she loved you," he murmured, his voice odd and husky. "Of course she did."

Then it was business again. "Princess, you've gotta get out of here, and you've gotta do it quick."

Had he struck her in the stomach? His words carried that great an impact.

"Get out of here?" she repeated.

"They've found you. By tonight they'll be knocking on doors."

"But I can't run away from here. I have no other place to go."

"Then you're going home."

That couldn't happen. It mustn't happen. She had come so far. She'd been so certain she was well hidden in this strange, unknown place—which she wouldn't have been able to find on a map. Yet in less than a week her father had found her. Her face must have registered dismay, because Ian looked concerned.

"You're not going to cry on me again, are you?" he asked.

A St. Ranganaux, even a female one, was of stronger stock than that.

Ian's eyes narrowed as he grasped her shoulders with

hands surprisingly gentle for a sturdy, substantial man. "I may have a solution," he declared. "It's not a very good one, but it's the only one I could think of."

She waited anxiously for him to continue. If he had a solution, any alternative, she had to hear it.

But, as always, breeding overrode even her survival instinct. "I would be interested in hearing that solution," she answered as indifferently as her royal breeding could manage.

"I'm not saying it's the *best* solution, mind you." He seemed uncomfortable with his solution.

"I don't need the best solution. I need *a* solution."

"Good answer. You just keep that in mind, Princess, while I try to explain this. OK?"

She nodded, anxious and waiting.

"I think we should leave—you and me, together," he began. "I think we should just climb in my car and get the hell out of here and see if we can shake these guys."

Katriana went numb with disappointment. Surely there was more to his plan, his solution, than just moving to another place to wait to be found again. These Pinkerton detectives, if they could track her so far in such a short time, must be veritable bloodhounds. Moving elsewhere would do nothing but delay the inevitable. In her imagination, Katriana had expected perhaps . . .

What, in truth, had she expected? Blazing guns? Trains roaring through violent storms in the night, toward unknown destinations? A stint with the circus? Americans were innovative, exciting people. Could this American man not improvise something a bit more venturesome than driving somewhere else in his car?

"Is that it?" she asked. She was afraid her voice echoed her dismay at his lame solution. "Is that your plan? I don't see how it can make much difference. I will still be caught eventually."

Why, at that very moment, did his eyes light up and decide to twinkle? His smile broke through—dimples and all, transforming his concerned look into something that caused her heart to flutter with ferocious abandon.

She preferred that he not smile and glow like that in her presence. Her circumstances were grave enough without the added distress of numerous vital parts fluttering out of control, and operating at lower—or perhaps higher—than usual energy levels.

"Well, Princess, would you think it might make any difference—"

"What did you say?" she snapped at him when she realized she had missed the last part of his silly rant. Surely she hadn't heard what she thought she had just heard. Surely the man hadn't finished with . . .

"—if we were married?"

"Married?" she squeaked.

The poor girl looked panic-stricken, as if he'd threatened her, not offered to marry her. Ian didn't like that at all. He'd made a serious offer and Princess Katriana appeared to be on the verge of throwing up.

"Yes, married," he repeated, more stern than he'd intended. He found himself immensely pissed off at her reaction, as well as with his own meddlesome stupidity. Hellfire! He didn't want to marry anybody either, but at least he could see the logic of it.

What logic? Who was he kidding? There was nothing the least bit logical about it. It was a harebrained, tomfool idea that made him look like a bigger idiot than he actually was. All he really wanted was *out of here*—and to stay single forever. He seemed to have developed an unfortunate case of hoof-in-mouth disease.

47

"Isn't marriage what I'm trying to avoid?" The princess was still squeaking. And about to hyperventilate.

"Hell, it was just a suggestion," he growled, irritated, almost hurt, that she was so distressed at his proposal; yet at the same time he was relieved that he hadn't yet heard that dreaded word *yes*. "And not a very good one, evidently. I didn't realize I was the dogfaced boy. Sorry about that."

He turned to leave and strode angrily toward the door. He figured a fair amount of stomping around was indicated here so he did that too. Damned snooty woman! He was embarrassed. No reason to act like he'd just pointed a gun at her head. For all she knew, maybe his proposal wasn't even a serious one. Maybe he was kidding.

Maybe he wasn't kidding.

And if he weren't kidding, what the devil had happened to his brain? Repeated knocks against a concrete wall must have turned it to mush. He *hated* the idea of being married. He hated the idea of even pretending to be married. And he hated the idea of spending even another minute with this woman, this *princess*.

She affected him. She aroused him. Physically, emotionally, every damned way she could arouse him. He needed to leave the room, to get away from her, and certainly not *marry* her.

Maybe he should thank God that she *didn't* want to marry him, no matter how briefly. She was annoying as hell. Or maybe he was just in a bit of a snit over the fact that she was peering down her royal nose at him.

"What is a dogfaced boy?" she queried before he could slam the door behind him.

He swung back around to face her again. "It's just something that we say sometimes. It means ugly, unattractive."

"You are not ugly and unattractive."

"Well, that's real nice to know. Thanks." He hoped she picked up on the sarcasm.

"I do appreciate your offer, Monsieur Grayson, but marriage is so—so permanent." She shrugged her fetching little shoulders.

"I hadn't planned for it to be *permanent.*"

"Not permanent?" She sounded shocked.

"Well . . . no," he stuttered. And waffled. And noticed that he sounded stupid.

"How is a marriage not permanent?"

"Is this some kind of religious problem you've got, Princess?" he muttered, his tone awash with a dreadful combination of alarm (at the mere thought of a prolonged marriage *to anybody*) and suspicion (of her motives, whatever they might be). Surely she realized that marriage between them would be nothing but a ruse, arranged to avert her forced marriage to some guy old enough to be her grandfather. He wasn't pledging his life to her. Hell, he barely knew her.

"I find you very strange, almost frightening, Monsieur Grayson," she whispered, her eyes—huge, dark pools of uncertainty—holding his gaze. He had to admit she was good. She was damned near perfect at her frightened-little-waif act. If the tabloids hadn't informed him so well of the mating habits of members of Mediterranean royal families, he might even have believed her. Despite all his vast, new-found knowledge of Mediterranean royalty, his heart experienced a painful little palpitation.

Nevertheless, the tone of their conversation had changed abruptly, growing somber and serious. He quit stomping. He let go of the edge of the door he was about to slam shut behind him and stared down at her.

"My life is not a joke," she continued. "I thought perhaps you had a serious solution, but I see you do not. You may leave now." Imperious to the bitter end, Katriana returned his stare. She looked haunted and fragile enough to crumble, and so beautiful that he could barely draw breath.

"It wasn't a joke, and I'm certainly not joking about the mess you're in," he protested. "I would never do that. My offer was serious. I just don't hold marriage in such high regard as you do. My one experience with it was not good."

"You have been married?"

"Yes, I was married once."

She seemed to ruminate on that fact, to consider it from numerous perspectives.

"But then, surely you know that we cannot marry. No Catholic priest would marry us, Monsieur."

"I guess not." He shrugged, wavering in between relief and disappointment, then turned again toward the door. "It's been nice knowing you, Princess. Sorry I couldn't help you but that's the way it happens sometimes. Good luck in—"

"But it *would* be legal?"

What the hell was she babbling about now?

"Pardon?" he asked, rather politely he thought, considering the absurdity of their conversation.

"Even though the Church would not recognize it, the marriage would be legal. Am I correct about that?" Princess Katriana was warming to the subject with every word she spoke.

"Of course," he agreed foolishly, as if he too were warming to the subject. No matter what he had suggested, for whatever convoluted reason he had fashioned to rationalize it in his own mind, the thought of any kind of marriage made him sick to his stomach. "Yeah, if you're legally married to me, your father can't make you marry the old guy."

"*Très bien.*" She nodded. "*C'est possible.*"

He nodded. He hoped he looked wise, but he felt incredibly foolish.

"A civil marriage only. Unconsummated, of course."

"Of course." *What the hell did that have to do with anything?*

"Perhaps that would be acceptable."

"It's your call, Princess. You're the one with the problem. I'm just a guy with some spare time on his hands. If you've got a better idea how to get yourself out of this mess, then go for it. You're not doing me any favors with this marriage. I'm the one doing the favor, you know." He felt the need to point that out to her. She had the most annoying habit of seeming to bestow a courtesy simply by participating in a two-way conversation. He shuddered to think of all the ways she might skew the real purpose behind a marriage between them.

"So we shall leave this place?" she moved quickly on to her next thought, now that she had evidently weighed the logistics of marrying a stranger.

"That's the plan." He shrugged but doubted his shrug was anywhere near as fetching as hers was.

"When?"

"Soon. Later today, if you can get ready that soon. How does that sound?"

She cleared her throat. "Please understand that I am not foolish, Monsieur Grayson. I do realize that I should not be leaving with you, traveling, with a stranger. But I will not—I cannot go back. *C'est impensable.*"

He must have looked as confused as he felt at whatever she'd just said, because she translated. "Unthinkable. Going back now would be unthinkable."

"Sometimes I growl and bark, Princess, but I'm pretty harmless," he tried to assure her. Surely to God she didn't think he would harm her.

"Don't think that I have forgotten last night, when you

said you were not to be trusted," she continued undaunted. "Though it seems that now, Monsieur Grayson, I must do that very thing. I must somehow trust you. But I am watching you every minute, aware of your every move."

And just what does a little bitty thing like you intend to do if I decide to step out of line? he wondered, but kept it to himself. He would strive to be a model of decorum. He did have impeccable manners when the situation called for them. And he could—probably—behave himself and keep his hands off her if he really tried, married or not.

Poor Princess Katriana was in desperate need of a knight in shining armor. What she had ended up with was only a poor, worn-out excuse for one. But maybe he was better than nothing.

Or—God help them both—maybe not.

Chapter 4

Katriana St. Ranganaux was the most infuriating woman Ian had ever known. And the nosiest. To be fair about it, maybe she was just inquisitive. But whatever her proper description, she was driving him crazy.

Like a child, her favorite word was "why." *"Pourquoi."* Finally he suggested that she quit speaking French. He didn't know any damned French and didn't care to. She was in the United States, and if she had any notion of sticking around for very long, she had better lose the French and start speaking English.

It hurt her feelings, of course, and he was sorry about that, but God Almighty! Enough was enough. There was something about her peppering her conversation with those odd little French words that kept every single particle of him on edge—all the time. Hearing those breathy French syllables from her luscious lips, watching her exquisite mouth form the exotic words, he was rapidly developing an embarrassing, *noticeable* physical need to kiss those lips, that mouth, to hold her tight against him, to bury his hungry body inside her.

Jesus! He needed to get a handle on his reactions—immediately! It would be insanity to let himself jump in bed with a blue-blooded princess who had, no doubt, slept her way up and down the royal bloodlines of the world.

No way would her royal highness ever allow such a catastrophe to happen either. He was nothing but a *good ol' boy,* born and bred in the North Carolina piedmont, who had been very lucky. For a little while anyway. Katriana was so much his opposite that it amazed him they could breathe the same air.

While he weighed these profundities, her infernal questions continued.

"Why must I leave all of my things here?" she asked with huge and soulful eyes.

"So when they track you here, and I assure you they will, they'll find your stuff still scattered around—" he frowned at the new batch of clutter that had materialized since his cleaning frenzy the night before "—and figure that you've just stepped out and will be back before too long. The dicks—excuse me, the *detectives*—will hang around here for a while waiting for you and we'll be that much farther away."

He knew right away he should have phrased it differently, because it made her smile. Her face lit up like a Christmas tree and he went mushy as a glob of Play-Doh.

That was not part of the plan.

The one fact she never questioned, however, was the convoluted logic behind her need to marry him. He'd hoped that she would challenge it, because there was a decent chance that she could talk him out of it. It was a lousy plan, doomed to backfire and ruin the lives of everyone involved. But the longer he pondered it, the more logical it seemed to become, which said little for his reasoning process.

If one ignored that marriage to a non-U.S. citizen without some sort of consent . . . or approval . . . or something . . . was probably not even legal, it almost made sense. He could protect her from her father. As long as she was legally married to him—or even as long as the rest of the world was trying to figure out if she was legally married to him—she would not be free to marry anyone else.

The Runaway Princess

Of course, if Katriana really wanted to avoid a forced annulment by her daddy, there was always the problem of *consummation*. The lady for sure had her own definite ideas on the subject. If the need arose, they might declare that they had been together, and then dare anybody to disprove it.

As a last-ditch, alternative, in case the unthinkable should happen and the whole misbegotten plan fall apart and crumble to the point of truth or dare, he had not the slightest doubt that he could rise to the occasion on a moment's notice and consummate the hell out of it.

"Why do you not have a job?" she asked him later, after they'd adjourned to his place so he could pack. Katriana had insisted on bringing along a small bag full of the essentials she was certain she couldn't live without.

Dealing with this woman was plain weird! Why wasn't she thrilled for him to ride off into the sunset with her, protect her, even assure her that along the way he'd buy her all the clothes and anything else she might need? But Katriana accepted it as her due, as if it were her right. That rather ticked Ian off. So did her asking about why he didn't have a job.

"Well, I kind of have a job but I don't work at it right now," he answered. Maybe he did and maybe he didn't still have a job. Nobody had ever bothered to confirm his employment status one way or the other. Benny Lamont, his boss and the owner of the racecar he drove had called to check on him. But old Benny sure hadn't bothered to ask when, or if, he would be able to start driving again.

The young driver Benny had found to drive in his place wasn't faring any worse, or better, than Ian had done before the wreck, which didn't say much for the accomplishments of either. If Benny would part with enough money to build a

55

decent car, then put an engine in it that didn't blow up halfway through the race, the final results might be a little better. But with his job, his entire career, and everything else that meant anything to him hanging in jeopardy, he decided this might not be the best time to make that suggestion.

"What kind of a job do you have?" she wondered, ever curious—or nosy. He was having trouble deciding which.

"I drive a racecar," he admitted. There'd been a time when he'd been proud of his work, but now he wasn't sure how he felt about it.

Katriana's eyes sparkled. She clapped her hands together. Ian was feeling pretty darned perky over his career choice until she uttered the one dreaded word that managed to deflate the poor, shredded remnants of his ego. "Monaco!"

"No," he said. Actually, it was more of a growl. "Not Monaco."

"But—?" She never finished her question, if indeed it was a question. After that one brief syllable, he cut her off.

"I don't race Formula One. I race stock cars—big cars like you see on the street."

"Do they go fast?" she wondered.

"Yes, Princess, they go fast. They go *real* fast."

She looked confused. Against his better judgment, he plopped her down on the couch in front of the television. "We should get on the road and out of here, but first I want to show you something."

He popped a tape into the VCR, a tape he had watched many times. All those years of granting interview after jovial interview—even when he was exhausted, much too busy, furious, half-sick, en route to the bathroom or any combination of these difficulties—had finally paid off. A pit reporter friend of his had sent the tape of the race in which he'd wrecked. It was, perhaps, his last link to a way of life he might never regain. He treasured it. It comforted him, yet at the same time told a terrifying story. He had sat alone before the television replaying this tape so many times that he had nearly worn it out.

The action picked up in the middle of the tape, but Ian immediately hit the rewind button. He knew exactly how far back to take it.

"There," he said. He pushed the play button—and felt the sweat rise, felt the nausea set in.

It made no difference how many times he watched it. He was always hit with the same sweaty, sinking feeling of looming death. As he watched himself racing on that perfect February day at Daytona, he could dredge up no memory whatsoever of what had transpired.

"See how fast we go?" he noted as he slid in beside her on the couch.

"*Oui,*" she murmured, caught up in the action.

"That's me in the black-and-orange car. See it? Right . . . there."

On the screen two cars, Ian's black and orange Ford and a bright, cherry-red Pontiac, sped side by side through Daytona's broad, sweeping, high-banked turns. Ian could sense the speed, feel the prickles of raw energy run through his hands, his feet, even his backside. As the car roared around the monster track, his reflexes slid into autopilot, informing him exactly when to turn the wheel, how much to turn it, when to brush the brake pedal because another car had shot too close in front of him. But no backing off the throttle. Never at Daytona. Do that even once, while the green flag is flying, and you might as well load everything up and get started for home.

Daytona's speeds were so dangerously high that the sanctioning body had mandated restrictor plates, metal plates that restricted the airflow into the carburetor and, as a result, the engine's horsepower. It worked well for its intended purpose, to keep the speed just under the 200-mile-per-hour mark. But the tradeoff was a long, dangerous, freight-train-like pack of cars running flat out, foot to the floor, nose to tail, scant inches apart, all powerless to summon that extra burst of horsepower necessary to avoid each other if the need arose. And ultimately, at some time during the race, that need arose.

That was why he now sat on a couch watching what would probably be written down in the record books as his last race and sweating like a sick racehorse.

He tried to pull himself back together enough to explain to Katriana, but it was hard to tell how much of it she actually understood. She seemed interested in the race itself, which Ian took as a positive sign that he wasn't boring the hell out of her. Thank God, she also seemed oblivious to his current attack of nerves.

"OK, now pay attention and watch what happens in a minute." She watched carefully, engrossed in the events unfolding on the screen.

The red Pontiac moved over closer to the side of the black and orange Ford, whose back-end wiggled almost imperceptibly.

"What we're doing there is not a wise action at Daytona. One of us should be behind the other, drafting, so we can both go faster. But Reggie wanted past me and I guess he thought he could do it."

Ian's black-and-orange Ford pulled ahead of Reggie's car, but by no more than a nose.

"I had him—right there. See that? I had the line and he couldn't do it. Right about . . . *there*, he realized he'd never get past me so he tucked in right behind me. Like that. See?"

The red car drifted back and did indeed pull in directly behind Ian's. Then it inched closer and closer until it bumped squarely into the rear bumper of Ian's car. Once. Twice.

"Oh, *non*," Katriana murmured. "He is wrecking you."

"No, he's not," Ian assured her. "What he did there is OK. That's called bump-drafting and he was trying to help me pick up a little speed so the airflow behind my car would pull him along faster too. It looks nasty, but it's not."

The back end of Ian's car wiggled noticeably at the exact instant Reggie burst forward for yet another bump.

"The back end got loose right there. It might have been slick tires, or some oil on the track, or maybe I just screwed up a little. It's hard to tell. You can see he was aiming again for the middle of my back bumper, but the back end of my car was still out of shape and he hit way to the left of where he was aiming."

The force of the blow knocked the back of Ian's car around to the right and the car commenced an amazingly slow, even graceful, turn, with the rear of the car leading the way. Still moving tail-first, and at tremendous speed, the car slid up the high-banked curve toward the outside wall. The move appeared almost elegant, like an ice-skater's lazy spin, until the doomed car hit the wall tail first, bounced off and turned around another full revolution . . .

. . . which brought its broadside squarely in the path of the oncoming chain of cars roaring toward it at full speed. The first car was already there, with no place to turn. It T-boned Ian's car in the driver's seat, whipping the vehicle on its side and sending it into a vicious series of barrel rolls. The other oncoming cars fanned out in an effort to avoid the wreck.

Some of them did, and some of them didn't.

At least three more cars, maybe more—it was difficult to

tell in the smoke and confusion—hit Ian's demolished car, sending what was left of it spinning around like a clumsy top, back and forth across the racetrack. It ricocheted off other cars and then the outside wall like a banked pool shot.

What finally came to rest low on the apron of the track, as the speedway curved into the first turn, no longer resembled a car. It might easily have been mistaken for a pile of discarded scrap metal. Ian marveled yet again that the mess of crushed metal had contained his still-living body.

Once again, he watched the frantic flagman wave the red flag to stop the race. Again he watched the pace car bring the line of slow-moving vehicles down pit road to a full stop. Again he watched the safety attendants rush to quench the fingers of fire creeping around his ruined car, then use an array of fearsome-looking tools to further demolish the car and pull what was left of him from it. His unconscious body was transferred to the waiting ambulance, which took him straight to a helicopter for the direct flight to the hospital. No interim stop for him that day at Daytona's infield care center.

Once again he watched interviews with many of the drivers—his best friends in the world—as the network filled up air-time while the race was delayed for cleanup.

Ian could recite every word of the report, but he watched it all again with Katriana so she could understand what he did and why he wasn't currently doing it. He forced himself to endure every last second of the tape, until the race started again, and life went on without him.

"Ian, *c'est horrible*," Katriana murmured, and turned toward him as he shut off the VCR. There might have been tears in her eyes, but he wasn't sure. He didn't look at her that close. He didn't dare.

He responded with a shrug. What could he say? In any event, he couldn't trust his voice not to quaver or break.

"Are you all right? I mean *really* all right?" she asked.

"Yeah, probably," he grunted, still refusing to look straight at her. He was afraid those aquamarine eyes of hers might be brimming with pity. He could stand a lot of things—pain, failure, even finality—but under no circumstances could he tolerate pity.

"It's a miracle you can walk," she marveled in a whisper. "It's a miracle you're even alive."

She touched his hair. She moved on to his forehead, trailing a curious, incredibly soft finger down the side of his cheek, to the corner of his mouth. Whether she meant for it to be that way or not, it was a tender, caring gesture, like that of a mother comforting a child.

Ian had to admit that it was indeed comforting, but at the same time it was troubling. And it scared him at least as much as watching the replay of his wreck. It felt as if she cared—as if for some reason she cared deeply about him—and he didn't like it. He didn't want to be cared for because he might be expected to care back, and he doubted he was capable of doing so. He had lived too long without love and was out of practice in all ways involving tenderness. For sure, he could show her royal highness one hell of a one-night stand if the chance arose, but anything more than that was too much to ask from a worn-out, used-up man with no future to speak of.

Yet he soaked up the touch of her hand like a desert soaking up rain. He ached for things that weren't his to have.

Katriana was too beautiful. She was too sympathetic. At the moment she needed his help too damned much. And she ought to have the sense to see what she was doing to him and keep her hands to herself.

But she didn't. Her wonderful hands explored his face, almost as if it might be the first time they had ever taken such

61

a liberty with any man's face. Her fingers brushed through his hair. Her eyes explored his face as insistently as her fingers had. When she swallowed, it was with difficulty.

God help me, I'm going to have to kiss her, he realized with dismay, and didn't like it one little bit. He had no business kissing her. He had no business even *wanting* to kiss her.

"You are a kind man," she murmured, oblivious to his distress. "And a very brave one."

That did it.

His mouth, feverish and needy, settled over hers. He found her strangely unreceptive, and his tongue had some persistent work to do to find its way into what he had expected to be an eager mouth. He delved and explored and got very little response except for the wild pounding of her heart against his chest. Baffled, he drew back and away from perhaps the least satisfying kiss in his long and illustrious kissing career.

Either the princess wasn't nearly as thrilled by that kiss as he had hoped she would be . . .

. . . or she had no idea how to kiss.

Chapter 5

As far as first kisses went, that one wasn't half bad.

Katriana was positive that she hadn't done it quite right, but it had happened so fast, before she could gather her wits. One minute Ian was gazing down at her politely, although she recalled his chocolate-brown eyes burning with a certain heavy-lidded glow, and the next minute his lips had settled over hers, his arms had wrapped around her, and his tongue had invited itself into her mouth.

Her head roared. Her heart pounded. Her whole body begged to wrap itself around him. Low inside her, something clenched in ecstasy.

When it was over, she shivered and tried to feign composure. Tried to catch her breath. She found kissing to be an alarming, intensely physical experience.

"I'm sorry," he muttered, dragging her back into the present. He looked annoyed.

She said nothing, but his words stung. Was he sorry for kissing her? Sorry for thrilling her so?

"I guess I misread the signs," he grunted, then eased himself up off the couch, stretching like a cat with a stiff back, and turned away. He rubbed one hand through his hair in the same unconscious gesture she had noticed more than once in their brief acquaintance.

"Why are you obsessed with your hair?" she asked, galloping off in a new and different direction, grabbing at any possible conversational straw, more in an effort to break the uncomfortable silence than in an attempt to hold a rational conversation.

"My hair?" he asked.

"*Oui,* your hair," she answered, relieved that he was following her lead.

Ian smiled, and Katriana's gaze dropped to his lips. Mere seconds ago those lips had kissed hers. They were disarming and bold, punctuated on each side with an appealing dimple. His smile was the smile of the devil himself.

"I guess I'm just glad to have it back. It was shaved off at the hospital," he explained, "to prepare me for some kind of brain surgery. Now I have to admit that I was asleep while all that was going on, but I fooled 'em and woke up before they got around to drilling a hole in my head."

"Woke up?"

"Yeah, woke up." He shrugged as if embarrassed. "I was unconscious for several days."

"Several days! *C'est horrible!*"

He shrugged again, perhaps to downplay the gravity of all that he'd endured. "I don't know much about that part of it. I was asleep."

"I'm sorry," she murmured, again overcome with shyness. Men, passion and tragedy were alien to her life. She had always been protected and shielded from them. Now she was being inundated with all three at once. A thumping heart and roaring blood were not conducive to witty conversation.

"No reason for you to be sorry. It wasn't your fault," he assured her.

Katriana decided then and there that she didn't like him polite. She liked him funny and irreverent, even bossy, as he had been the night before as he scurried about, tidying her quarters. Friendship with a man, any man, was yet another strange, new experience, and she had so enjoyed the comfortable, informal camaraderie that had grown between them the evening before.

But in the seconds since he'd kissed her, everything was changed. Different. That easy familiarity was gone. The mood between them was stilted and uncomfortable.

Had she reacted too strongly to his kiss? Or perhaps she had not reacted strongly enough?

The nuns had instructed her on the general workings of her body, along with certain basic aspects of the reproductive process. But not one of those nuns had had the foresight—or the courtesy—to mention that a man's touch could be so exhilarating. That it could curl her toes and leave her breathless. Nuns were not the most knowledgeable experts on the subject, but still, somebody should have been kind enough to warn her.

Monique, her other teacher—the one who *wasn't* a nun, the one who presumably was an expert on men—hadn't warned her either.

Katriana's father had employed Monique in anticipation of Katriana's marriage to Sir Christian, to instruct her in the various duties of a wife the nuns had overlooked. To her credit, Monique had worked diligently with her pupil—with the assistance of certain choice fruits and vegetables—to demonstrate the actual mechanics of the physical acts that the elderly Sir Christian might expect from his young wife.

"Anyway, Princess, I'm not that easily offended," Ian drawled, dragging her once again back to the present. His expression was blank, yielding no clue to his real feelings. His eyes were guarded, quite unlike those same eyes just moments before, magnetic and brimming with fire, when he had kissed her. She did believe that in some way she *had* offended him or at least caused him discomfort, because she noticed he called her "Princess" when he seemed uncomfortable.

Katriana *hated* it when he called her *Princess*. Not only was his form of address improper, it showed a lack of respect.

"Well, *I* am *quite* easily offended," she snapped at him.

Ian shot to attention. "I beg your pardon."

"Don't call me *Princess*," she instructed. "Do I call you *racer?*"

He arched an eyebrow, in disbelief perhaps, but said nothing.

"If you are so intent on calling attention to my lineage, then you should call me *Your Highness*. Though that term is—"

"Your Highness," Ian enunciated, and inclined his head in a show of respect, or more probably disrespect.

"As I was saying before I was so *rudely* interrupted," she continued, a frosty chill creeping into her voice, "that is the formal term, and rarely used outside of state affairs."

"So I can't call you *Princess* and I shouldn't call you *Your Highness*. Just what, *exactly*, may I call you?"

"My name is Katriana, and that is what I wish to be called."

"Well, *Katriana*." The man put far more emphasis on that one word than was polite. "Have you considered that the very first time I call you Katriana in public, the jig is up? That about a hundred Pinkerton detectives will jump out of the bushes, probably shoot me right through my black heart, and you'll be back having tea with Daddy and Sir Christian before you can say, *Who shot J.R.?*"

"Who . . . shot . . . J.R.?" she repeated, perplexed. "The Pinkerton detectives shot somebody?"

"Figure of speech, Prin—I mean Katriana." He again rubbed a hand through his hair again and muttered some curse, the precise meaning of which eluded her.

"Like a noun?" she wondered, trying to understand.

"No. A noun is a *part* of speech. A *figure* of speech is something you say that doesn't really mean what it says. It means something . . . well . . . something different."

"What does that have to do with someone named J.R. getting shot?"

"Nobody named J.R. really got shot."

"Hmm . . . so who is this J.R. anyway?"

"Listen to me," Ian instructed. "There is no J.R. Nobody got shot. It's just something we say, so forget it. Okay?"

"Why would you say something like that?"

"We just do, that's all. We Americans are weird like that. Just forget about J.R.!"

She shrugged.

"And I'm not going to call you Katriana," Ian continued as if the issue were somehow connected with J.R.'s being shot . . . or not shot . . . or whatever happened to J.R., whoever he was. "I think I'll call you Katie."

"Katie?" she shrieked. It was an ugly, raucous sound, and she did not care to be the one responsible for having produced it. She'd never shrieked before in her life. Not ever. But this man was infuriating. "Why would you call me Katie? My name is—"

"From now on, your name is Katie."

"Since we seem to be acquiring new names, why don't I call you . . . oh, how about *Elvis?*"

"Honey, you can call me Uncle Tater-Blossom if it makes you happy, but I don't see any point to it. You're the one trying to hide from your daddy and the whole Pinkerton detective force," Ian pointed out.

"Oh."

"*Oh,* is right. Now, Katie, isn't there something you'd like to say to me?"

He stood his ground in front of her, awaiting an apology for her show of bad manners. She couldn't dispute that he deserved one. But what he got was something else entirely.

She stuck her tongue out at him.

Never before in her life had she done such a depraved thing. Never before in her life had she ever even *wanted* to do such a depraved thing. Never before in her life had there ever been anyone who justified such ill-bred behavior.

Ian was shocked. She could tell by the way his whole body stiffened, by the way his eyebrows shot up. But the man spent scarcely a second considering her audacity before he commented, "And just where was that pretty little tongue a couple of minutes ago when I was kissing you, trying to find it?"

Embarrassed, she reclaimed her wayward tongue and quickly snapped it up inside her mouth.

"Next time I kiss you, lady—and I assure you that there *will* be a next time—you might want to try doing that during the kiss, not afterwards. I can just about guarantee that you'll enjoy it a lot more that way." He wagged his eyebrows for a little added emphasis.

As he wandered off back into his bedroom to finish packing—or so he claimed—Katriana heard him muttering to himself. Something incomprehensible about God saving him from frigid women.

Her English was not perfect, but she was certain that *frigid* referred to something very, very cold. She had no idea what he was talking about.

Certainly not her! At the moment, she was feeling quite warm.

Ian was accustomed to spending much of his time alone. For that reason, he found the prospect of the eight-hour drive from Daytona Beach to Atlanta, cooped up in the car with Katriana—with *Katie*—frightening. Almost unbearable. That was the official reason.

The unofficial reason was something else. Her nearness bothered him. Her unique scent, as sweet and heady as jungle blossoms, or maybe heaven. Her legs encased in some kind of silky designer slacks that whispered as she moved. Her perky little breasts thrusting forward and jiggling around in a sleeveless sweater that had probably cost more than his recent hospital bill. Every single thing about this woman drove him wild.

He listened as she tried to keep from peppering her conversation with French. He watched her try to mask her fear as the fragile framework of her ill-conceived plan crumbled around her. Through it all, her delicate back remained ramrod straight. She couldn't quite mask the fear in her eyes when she allowed them to seek him out, but no hint of that fear spilled over into her voice. Throughout what must have been for her a life-shattering ordeal, she appeared serene and composed.

He observed these things out the corner of one eye, as he watched Interstate 75 unwind before them into the night. And he asked himself a hundred times, *Whatever possessed me to get involved in this mess?*

"Your car is very excellent," she announced into the thick, dark silence, practicing her new method of driving him crazy. Ever since he had requested that she eschew French, Katriana had commenced dropping somewhat incorrect words into her speech. He knew these lapses were not intentional. But they underscored her vulnerability—and that she was so very different from him, so very wrong for him and whatever life he could offer her.

He must be a freakin' idiot to even be considering offering

her any sort of life at all. Not that he really *was* considering such a future, but . . .

Geez!

"Thank you," he muttered through gritted teeth. "Somehow I just knew you were the kind of gal who could appreciate a good Porsche. I must be psychic."

Until his wreck, Ian had loved his Porsche with the sort of passion he usually reserved for women. Since the wreck he'd debated whether to sell the damned thing and go in for something with more ground clearance, something a six-foot-two-inch guy could get in and out of, and sit in, without bending his aching back or cramping his bum leg.

Katie—he *must* learn to think of her as Katie—laughed and Ian was overwhelmed with visions of angels and tinkling harps. She shifted around to look at him and he got another delicious whiff of her perfume.

His body tightened intimately and he squirmed around in his seat to ease the pressure building inside his jeans. That was exactly what he *didn't* need. Life was complex enough already as he sped through the night with the damned Runaway Princess herself.

"Where are we going?" Katriana flounced around in her seat, but Ian doubted that she was twitching from the same sexual desire that pounded through him. At the moment she seemed angry with him. So he'd neglected to tell her where they were headed. Big damned deal.

"I thought we'd head up to Atlanta for a few days, get lost in the crowd, then . . . well . . . we'll just play it by ear after that."

"Ah, Atlanta." She relaxed visibly. "I know Atlanta. I have once traveled to Atlanta."

"Let me guess. You were there for the Olympics."

"*Oui.* Yes, it was most indeed for the Olympics," she answered, once again butchering the English language. But

Ian barely noticed. He was too busy trying to drive while watching her magnificent hair swish across one bared shoulder when she cocked her head to one side. He felt a delicious need to groan, but decided he better not. Poor Katie had enough troubles at the moment without receiving positive proof that her new acquaintance was lusting after her.

"Told you I was psychic," he grunted. But he tried to soften it with a slight smile.

"You are *très* naughty, I believe," she lectured. "I think you read of my trip to Atlanta in one of your newspapers."

"So you think you're important enough to make the newspaper, do you?"

"But of course." She swished her hair around again and Ian's entire body clenched. Who would have guessed that hair could be such a turn-on? "Americans are obsessed with royalty."

He watched her lift her perfect little nose at the thought of heathen Americans daring to invade her royal privacy by reading of her escapades.

He gave an impolite snort at the thought of being obsessed with royalty. "You sure do flatter yourself."

"How so?"

"To assume I have either the time or the inclination to read the supermarket rags and follow you and your shenanigans."

"Shenanigans?" She puzzled over the word.

He swore under his breath. Holding a meaningful conversation with Katriana was like trying to communicate with a three-year-old.

"You are unkind to swear in my presence," she informed him, crossing her arms.

"Sorry," he muttered.

"I should think so." Then, "So, tell me, what is a shenanigan?"

"Dumb things. Ditzy stuff."

She swished her hair around some more and expelled an elegant huff. "I have never *shenaniganed* in all of my life."

"Whatever you say," he grunted in disbelief.

The temperature in the car seemed to drop ten degrees. Outrage oozed from her every pore. She wouldn't look at him, as if she'd rather stare at the black nothingness of the South Georgia night than tolerate the sight of him.

To bring matters back into some sort of sync, he made a polite suggestion. "You about ready for a pit stop?"

Eyes wide with questions and perhaps still some leftover annoyance, she inquired a tad frostily, "What is a pit stop?"

"Gas, a cup of coffee, the bathroom—you know—"

"No, indeed, I do not know. I have never pit-stopped in my life," she said. "Besides, we do not make use of public facilities."

Ian laughed out loud.

"I do not see the—"

"Well then I hope your royal bladder is king-sized—"

"One never discusses one's organs," she spat, her hair bouncing around as visible proof of her irritation. She had magnificent hair, and she wasn't afraid to use it to punctuate her speech.

"—because we're still five hours from Atlanta," he finished.

"Oh," she murmured, and her face fell.

"We'll find a nice, clean place, and everything will be just fine," he assured her. He even patted her hand. It was soft but cold. The poor girl must be scared to death. So, being the gentleman that he was, he held on to that hand, just to warm it, of course.

He watched her weigh her options, which were few, as far as he could see.

She was still considering those options several minutes later when he piloted the Porsche off the interstate highway and pulled into a well-lit service station. He noticed her almost nibble at the corner of her thumbnail, then catch herself before committing the lapse in etiquette. Glimpsing her vulnerability in yet another unguarded moment quelled any urge to laugh he might have had.

To Katriana, this must be a severe problem, something she had never before encountered, and it underscored how very different she was from every other woman he had known. It reinforced how much she needed someone, at the moment *him,* to guide her through the perils of life beyond the royal enclave. But how did one coach a princess on the protocol of something so basic as the use of a public restroom?

And there were problems besides the potty that he had neglected to consider.

In a quick stopgap attempt to solve the worst of them, he reached around behind him into what passed for the backseat of his Porsche and grabbed a cap. That cap was, of course, black and orange, the colors of his racecar, and bore his sponsor's name.

"Here." He handed it to her.

She stared at it, not daring to touch it, and even sniffed at it as if testing it for noxious odors.

"Yes, it's been on my head," he confessed. "But I swear I don't have lice or any other kind of cooties. You can even check." He offered his head for her inspection.

"What am I supposed to do with this?" she asked.

"Put it on. Wear it."

"Wear it?"

"Yes, *Katie.*" He made a point of emphasizing her new name. "Wear it. Put it on, pull your hair up and stick it out the hole in the back, and pull the bill down low over your eyes

73

like . . . this." He, of course, did it all for her. He even made a gallant effort to sweep her hair up and out the opening in the back, as he had watched other women do. That was a little trickier than it looked, but the end result wasn't awful . . . well, it wasn't *too* awful. He added the finishing touch of a pair of aviator sunglasses from his glove box.

His mission was accomplished. The lady who stood before him looked nothing like Princess Katriana.

The indignity of it all!

To be instructed in such personal and delicate matters, in the middle of the night, standing beside a petrol pump. She wrinkled her nose at the stench from the fuel as Ian went about filling the car's tank, then took a quick look around to be sure that no one was near enough to have witnessed her shameful lapse of *décorum*. Making faces, wearing disguises. So unlike anything she had ever done before. *Bonne chance* was on her side for once, because no other car or person was visible, or even present, in the station lot. Just an abundance of bright lights, petrol pumps waiting for customers, and Ian lecturing about *dangereux* strangers, the various available petrol grades, and *toilettes publiques*.

All her life, Katriana had been instructed that bodily functions were never to be discussed or alluded to, and certainly never performed where one could be observed. One *went* before one left for one's scheduled activities and waited to go again until one returned to the palace. Such things were taken into account when the schedules were prepared.

But these Americans! Ian insisted that she use the public facility.

She was humiliated.

"I understand these places are unclean," she declared.

"Well, don't touch anything."

"Will other people be present?"

"I have no idea."

And on and on to the one question that she was the most embarrassed to ask. But who else could advise her on such a critical issue?

"If one does not touch anything, how does one . . . go about it?"

Ian was no help at all. "You're on your own with that one. I don't have a clue," he said. "Squat over it, maybe?"

She wished he had kept that suggestion to himself.

So, wearing Ian's hat and his sunglasses (at midnight, no less) she waited close beside him, watched him fill the fuel tank with petrol, then walked with him across the oil-spattered tarmac toward the station. Strange, unknown night birds called to each other in the distance, but the rumble of trucks in the darkness drowned their cries. America was so intense! By all rights, she ought to feel lost in its vast wilderness. But she didn't. Instead she felt exhilarated, and for the first time in her life, a heady sense of freedom stirred inside her.

"OK, stay right beside me while I pay for the gas," Ian counseled. Then he led her inside and paid the cashier. She noticed the way his gaze swept the station lot, the building as they entered it, even the cashier's face.

"Now," he said as he turned them toward the restrooms, "you go on in and . . . do whatever . . ." He charitably omitted any specifics. "And I'll stay right here by the door and wait for you."

Although the door appeared to be clean enough, she was not enthusiastic about touching it, pushing it . . .

"Wait a sec," Ian cautioned her. Then he pushed the door open and craned his neck around to peek into the ladies' restroom.

"I don't think you're supposed to—" Katriana began.

But by then he had finished his inspection of the restroom. "Nobody in there," he announced. "I'm glad I had enough sense to check that out before you strolled in. I'm not much good at this cloak-and-dagger stuff yet, but I promise to improve as we go along." He held the door open for her to enter.

Face aflame, she marched in, took care of necessities, and even washed her hands with the acrid soap. It reminded her of the soap the kennel-keeper used to scrub her purebred hounds. The entire procedure took only a minute or two, and she found herself ridiculously proud to have accomplished such a simple feat.

She found Ian exactly where she had left him. His face lit up and he gave her an encouraging smile as she exited the restroom. At the sight of him, she felt her unsuspecting heart jolt in her chest, but she did her best to ignore it. She did not wish to be attracted to this man. She was forced, for the moment, to trust him with her safety, but to add her heart to the equation was more than she could manage.

But that didn't stop her from longing to run to him, to bury herself in his safe and substantial arms—unwise yearnings, considering who he was. He had committed himself to helping her escape her pursuers. He had even offered himself as a quasi-husband to thwart her father's scheme, but he had uttered not a word about caring for her. He seemed much too occupied battling his own demons to take on hers. He had offered his protection and his name, but nothing else. No permanence, no feelings, certainly no intimacy. She barely knew him well enough to call him by his first name.

But he was very kind. When she was with him, her problems felt diminished. And when he smiled at her—oh, my! It was like a surge of electricity. A burst of heat. Thunderous music.

"No problems?" he asked, oblivious to the cataclysm he had just set into motion.

"No problems," she confirmed.

"OK, now for the tricky part." He took her hand and led her to the magazine rack along the front wall. "Listen to me. You stay right here. Flip through a magazine. Don't move," he instructed. "I'm going to step into the men's room for just a minute. Okay?" He made direct eye contact with her, and almost seemed to be asking her permission, not giving instructions.

She nodded.

"Keep an eye on anybody who comes in here, and if anybody approaches you, go straight over to the clerk and stay right beside him until I get there. Understand?" He emphasized his words with a quick squeeze of her arm.

"I understand," she answered. "Is it that serious? Do you think someone is following us?"

"I don't know," he replied. "I doubt it, but I really don't know, and we can't take that chance."

She held his gaze, watched it heat up and smolder and then drop from her eyes to her lips. His own lips twitched as if he might be fighting a losing battle with himself not to kiss her.

"Here," he muttered, grabbing a magazine and jamming it into her hands. "Open this and act like you're reading it. Keep your head down, keep your cap pulled as far down over your eyes as you can, and stay in plain sight of the clerk. Are you gonna be okay?"

She nodded uncertainly.

"I'll be right back."

She nodded again. Then he was gone and she was alone.

Vulnerable as a newly hatched bird. Conspicuous. Looking ridiculous in the strange hat and sunglasses.

What was she doing here in this place, wherever it was, with this strange man? How unlike her to run away from her father—her heritage—and straight into the arms of a stranger. She and Ian Grayson had no common ground. No compatible culture. Every single thing about him and his country was alien to her. Yet he had offered to marry her, at least in name. To take care of her, protect her. And she was very close to agreeing to his offer.

Why? Because she trusted him instinctively, although she didn't care to pursue the matter of trust too far, too soon.

She also had trusted her father, yet he had betrayed her.

She blinked back tears. No doubt Ian would not want to come back and find her crying, standing in the middle of a petrol station, clutching a magazine and blubbering.

Why should it matter what he thinks? she challenged herself. She was a grown woman, a woman who had accomplished feats she would never have believed herself capable of doing, simply so she might control her own destiny.

She would get through this, with or without his help. He seemed a trustworthy sort, despite his protestations to the contrary. But did she dare turn her destiny over to this stranger? Which was the lesser of the two evils? Should she return to Île d'Arinedra and marry Sir Christian, or remain here with Ian and marry him, however briefly, for the convoluted reasons he had attempted to explain? She was quite certain that he found his reasons no more justifiable than she did. So why had he fashioned such a ludicrous plan in the first place? And why was she willing to go along with it?

The object of her musings pushed open the restroom door. His eyes sought her and she watched relief flood his face when he found her as he'd left her. For all the fear and uncertainty she had endured in those few minutes, her heart danced at the sight of him striding toward her.

"Want some coffee?" he offered.

"*Oui,*" she answered, not remembering until the word was spoken that she was supposed to be speaking English. "Yes," she amended. "Yes, please."

Ian gave her a quick smile, almost paralyzing in its intensity. He didn't mean it. She knew that. That devastating smile was his normal smile, the one he smiled at everyone. But, oh, *mon dieu!* She felt herself tottering between overwhelming fear and overwhelming attraction, knowing she would burn herself out if she couldn't find some kind of balance.

She watched him pour a large Styrofoam cupful of coffee. For the first time, she noticed how tired he looked and that he was limping slightly. Until that moment, she'd noticed no limp. She suspected he was able to control it until fatigue set in.

He started to pour a second cup of coffee from the pot, then changed his mind. He smiled to himself as he returned the pot to the burner and filled the second cup from a large metal dispenser sitting near the coffee pot.

"Here." He handed the second cup to her. "Surprise."

Ian took no cream or sugar in his coffee. He sipped it black, and piping hot.

Katriana's coffee appeared to be already creamed, which puzzled her because she'd watched Ian closely and he'd done nothing more than draw the coffee from the machine.

She took a tentative sip because she did not like the taste of American coffee. But she desperately needed something warm to hold in her freezing, trembling hands.

It was wonderful! It was . . .

"Cappuccino!"

"I thought you might like that. It's probably not like the royal cook and cappuccino-maker makes, but it's not too bad, is it?"

"It's very good. *Merci*," she thanked him as he paid the cashier for their coffees, then caught herself. "I mean, thank you."

"You are very welcome," he answered, again flashing his wicked smile. His voice rasped, low and husky. Every single part of her responded to that voice. The result was a visible shiver.

"Cold?"

"No. Not really."

He looked down at her, puzzled, until she gave him something else to think about.

"I will drive," she announced.

She could tell by the way he stiffened that Ian didn't like idea at all.

"Well, I'm not sure . . ." he began.

"You are not sure of what?" she asked, irritated. "Not sure that I can drive?"

"Well, no, not exactly."

"Not exactly what?"

He shrugged like a petulant little boy.

"You are incredibly tired. I am incredibly bored," she pointed out. "I see no problem."

"Have you ever driven anything before?"

"*Have I ever driven anything before?* What kind of a question is that?" she demanded. Despite her violent attraction to him, Ian brought out the worst in her. "*Of course* I have driven before. I have a driver's license. I have driven cars very much like this one. Cars even *better* than this one."

He pondered his dilemma, his brows furrowed together, his lips pursed. "Can you drive a five-speed transmission?"

"*Oui.*"

"Have you ever driven on a highway like that one?" He motioned in the direction of the interstate highway.

"*Oui.*"

"You're sure you have a driver's license?"

"*Oui.*"

"From where?"

"From my country, of course. Also honored in all of Europe."

"Do you drive much?"

"*Mais oui.* But of course. How do you think I get to where I am going?"

"Well, I never thought about that very much," he admitted. "I might have guessed you were chauffeured around in limousines."

"That too, of course," she was compelled to agree. "But sometimes I drive myself. Truly, I am a competent driver."

"Well, that's very interesting." Ian's attempt at polite conversation was no more than a ploy to kill time, to delay his inevitable decision of *yes* she could drive his car, or *no* he would not allow it.

"I will be so very most careful with your car," she promised, steering their exchange back to the subject at hand. "If I dent it, you can do something terrible to me. You can spank me," she offered, teasing him.

Ian's eyes glittered. His smile was back, dimples flashing daringly at her. The car keys dangled from his index finger. "Lady, I doubt that spanking would be much punishment for the likes of you. Don't you jet-set royal bed-hoppers do that to each other over drinks before dinner?"

He had lost her. She had no idea what he was talking about. What was a "jet-set" or a "bed-hopper"? She had heard of a "jet ski" and a "grasshopper," but neither word suited the context of his sentence.

While she strove to decipher his retort, Ian dropped the keys into her empty hand and folded her fingers around them. "If you mess up my car, I guess I'll just have to kiss you again," he muttered. "You sure as hell weren't too crazy about *that.*"

Ian never let anyone else drive his car. Not ever.

So why was he doing it now?

Because he was exhausted and the painkiller he needed made him sleepy. Katriana seemed a competent driver. She worked her way easily through the gears, all five of them, rolled up the entrance ramp onto the acceleration lane of the interstate and blended into the northbound traffic as if she had done it a million times.

"Watch the speed limit," he warned her. "This isn't the Autobahn, you know."

She took her eyes off the road long enough to give him a playful smile, and murmured a low, *"Oui, monsieur."* He recognized her teasing. He also felt it tingling like a shiver of electricity through certain unmentionable parts of him.

God, he hated it when he tingled! He hated being so damned susceptible to her appeal, so defenseless against her smile and all the rest of her. Women had their moments of usefulness, but the rest of the time they were nothing but a damned nuisance.

He shifted around in the unfamiliar passenger's seat in search a more comfortable position for his long legs and stiff back. Nothing felt right, so he continued to root around like a dog breaking in a new bed.

Eventually, he gave up and reached in his pocket for the bottle of pills, shook one out, and swallowed it dry. That wasn't the easiest way to take a pill, but it was tiny, his coffee was gone, and he'd be damned if he'd borrow a swig of her

82

cappuccino. Too personal . . . too intimate . . . too much like
a kiss. And she had made it quite plain that she wasn't interested in his kisses.

His next attempt at comfort was more successful, and
soon the painkiller, combined with his post-midnight exhaustion and the radio's soothing, late-night music, lulled him
toward sleep.

He expected to dream of Cheryl, his wife. That was usually what happened when he slept. Oh, she sure as hell wasn't
his wife any more, and these days probably wouldn't rouse
herself to spit on him if he was on fire, but once upon a
time . . . years ago . . .

Almost always in his sleep, Cheryl came to him again.
Eighteen again, vivacious, full of bounce and vitality, every
bit as crazy in love with him as he'd been with her. In his
dreams, she seldom spoke or did much of anything at all. She
simply *was*, and that was enough.

He refused to let himself to dream of the woman she'd
become, because it hurt too much. That would come under
the heading of a nightmare. Ex-wife or not, she should have
had more class than to seek him out, while he lay flat on his
back in the hospital, for the sole purpose of announcing that
she intended to collect in full her monthly alimony payments.
Too bad about his accident, she'd cooed, but she had her
own obligations . . . blah . . . blah . . . blah . . .

Cheryl now hated him with religious zeal, and the sad part
was that he didn't blame her. At one time, he'd tried to place
blame for their broken marriage on her shoulders because she
couldn't adapt to his success, didn't understand the demands
of his career. Or, failing that, he tried shifting the blame to the
nameless women who had passed through his life and his bed
as he traveled from track to track on the racing circuit.

But the true fault lay, of course, with him. He knew it, and had always known it. He had ruined a good marriage and turned a sweet, wonderful woman who had once loved him into a money-grubbing shrew.

Guys like him didn't get second chances, mainly because they didn't deserve them. He welcomed his dreams of Cheryl because he understood that a part of his punishment should be to dream of a woman he could never have because that woman no longer existed. He'd killed all the good and decent parts of her.

So, tottering on the edge of sleep, he waited for Cheryl to tiptoe in and torture him with more dreams of what should have been.

Instead, it was Katriana who shared his dream; her hair blowing loose and wild in a flower-drenched breeze, her laughter tinkling like a wind chime. She smiled at him until his knees were weak. She chattered to him but her words were incomprehensible. Frustrated, he wound his arms around her and kissed her enchanting mouth to stop the flow of unintelligible words, then lowered her to the ground until she lay beneath him.

She must have enjoyed the kiss more than the previous one because she opened her mouth invitingly. She melted against him.

"Katriana," he whispered against her hair. "Oh, God, Katriana . . ."

She shivered in his arms. "Ian," she responded. "Ian . . ."

"Ian! Wake up, Ian."

He jerked awake with such force that he bumped his head against the side window.

"Tell me again. What did you say I must do when we arrive at Macon?"

"Macon?"

"*Oui*, Macon. You said to do something when I got to

Macon, but now I cannot remember what."

"Macon?" he repeated, still fuzzy with sleep and arousal.

"*Yes,* Macon," she repeated, emphasizing the word *yes* instead of her usual *oui.*

"Macon," he repeated again, shaking his head to clear away the vivid vision of her in his arms, accepting his kisses. Returning them. "Macon. Take the bypass around Macon."

"*Merci,*" she thanked him, then cast him a quick, curious look. "Are you all right?"

"Oh, I'm just dandy," he muttered, and gave an exaggerated stretch. It was less a stretch than a ploy to allow him to move around in his seat and hide the embarrassing bulge in his jeans.

He hated being vulnerable, easy prey to his growing attraction to a woman who was wrong for him in every possible way. He knew he didn't belong in a serious relationship with any woman, especially not *this* one. He had proven himself unable to devote himself to any one woman—even if that woman happened to be his wife.

As for Katriana—merciful heaven! She was royalty. Not exactly the sort of woman who would be interested in a probably-unemployed minor celebrity from North Carolina who wasn't even interesting enough to make the supermarket scandal sheets.

So what was he doing entrenched in this mess? Why were they racing through the night, trying to lose a band of detectives intent on sending her back home to Daddy? Why hadn't he told her he had other priorities and she was on her own?

Because I'm a certified lunatic, that's why, he told himself. Because he was a sucker for a pair of turquoise eyes and a firm little behind. Because there was something in this woman that had reached out and tapped into a hidden pocket of chivalry deep down inside.

Because she was, perhaps, his last chance to do something right and decent for the benefit of someone other than himself.

Because in the short time he'd known her, she had turned his world upside down. And, on top of all that, it was possible that he had committed the one cardinal sin that could very well ruin his life far more than it already was. Because he was trying to—or more correctly, trying *not* to—fall in love with the most unsuitable woman for him that God had ever created.

Chapter 6

Atlanta was huge.

Much larger than Katriana remembered from her previous trip. As they approached the city, traveling up Interstate 75 from the south, she saw it materialize far off in the distance, bathed in soft morning light. Strange and magical, like the Land of Oz creeping up over the horizon.

Unlike the European cities she knew, which were steeped in history, Atlanta looked absurdly new. She wondered if it had any history at all. How could it? The skyline looked as if it had been built only the day before.

The long and tedious drive through the night ended, just in time for a breakfast of fried eggs, grits, biscuits and gravy.

Although Katriana would have much preferred a light *omelette de champignons* and some hot tea, she admitted that the fried eggs were not as *atroce* as they looked. But Atlanta's idea of gravy was nothing like her own. Even if one could force oneself to ignore its odd appearance, it was an abomination to serve gravy without benefit of a ladle. Ian used his own spoon as a makeshift ladle, serving each of them gigantic portions of the thick, white, pepper-flecked . . . whatever-it-was. It wasn't exactly a liquid, but it wasn't a solid either. One might just as easily spread it with a knife as serve it with a spoon. Left to her own devices, Katriana would have ignored it. The grits were completely inedible, and the gravy only made them worse.

As Ian watched her attempt to suppress a queasy shudder after her one and only mouthful of gravy-slathered grits, he kindly offered to buy her an antacid—which reminded him that they also needed to pick up a few other necessities.

For perhaps the first time in her life, Katriana was in no mood to shop. She glanced at her watch, aghast at Ian's suggestion that they shop so soon after breakfast. Did he not realize that only servants and workmen shopped before lunch?

She would have much preferred to find lodging so she could get some sleep, but Ian, who seemed to know all about such matters—and who had napped fitfully while she drove—declared it was too early in the morning to find suitable rooms. That made no sense at all to her, but she was in no position to argue. All she knew was that she had been a guest in the finest hotels in the world and that those rooms had always been ready whenever she arrived, no matter how early or late it was.

So now they stood in front of a K-Mart at a ridiculous hour on a steamy, late-August Atlanta morning.

What in the world is K-Mart? Katriana wondered. Was a "mart" not a small market? The brick building in front of her was like no "mart" she had ever envisioned. It was immense.

She thought the place was big and ugly, almost frightening. And Ian's mutterings about K-Mart princesses convinced her that despite his occasional kindnesses, Ian Grayson was the rudest of men.

"Welcome K-Mart shoppers," an overhead loud speaker blared.

Given the appearance of the inside, Katriana was not at all sure she cared to be a K-Mart shopper. She had shopped in the finest stores of Paris, London and Milan, but never in her life, had she seen a place like this. No carpeting. Clanging cash registers and *les employés* in full view of the customers. The air was ripe with the *mauvaise odeur* of buttered popcorn.

The lump of gravy in her stomach shifted unpleasantly.

"What size jeans do you wear?" Ian asked with no warning at all, and he seemed to expect an immediate answer. Did he not realize how complex such a question was, for someone accustomed to being measured for clothing only by dress-makers?

And what a strange concept, to pile all of one's purchases into a rolling metal cart—or basket, as Ian called it. The contraption looked nothing at all like a basket.

"We'll start with a size six, I think," he announced. "I've got a pretty good eye for that sort of thing." Then . . . plunk . . . the rolling basket was full of jeans. *Off the rack!* "Where's the dressing room?"

Fortunately, *dressing room* was a concept he understood . . . *until she saw it!*

It was no more than a cubicle! A wretched, tiny, unclean little cubicle with a sleazy cloth curtain hanging across the opening, the only barrier between her modesty and anyone wandering by. And there were no assistants. Not even one. How did one fit one's self for clothing? Who positioned the pins for alterations?

"I think we'll start with a medium top. It might be a little big in the shoulders but you've got yourself kind of a hefty chest there, young lady."

The man had been ogling her breasts! And was announcing his observations in public!

"I beg your pardon!" She tried to freeze him with her stare, but Ian was unfreezable.

"Sure." He winked at her and feigned innocence. "What did you do?"

Not only was he unfreezable—he was *detestable.* She elevated her nose and tried to ignore him.

Then, as if Ian had no idea how ill-mannered his lame attempt at humor had been, he began piling his rolling basket with an assortment of *personal* items. Toothbrushes, toothpaste, hairspray, shampoo, combs, brushes, unmentionables —*intimate feminine hygiene items.*

"I don't mind buying whatever we need," he declared, "but I'll be damned if I'll run out in the middle of the night for this kind of stuff."

Katriana was crimson with embarrassment by the time Ian finished his shopping expedition. On top of humiliating her almost beyond endurance, the man had abominable taste in lingerie. She would die a thousand deaths before she'd wear shocking red underthings, or dare to sleep in that big, green whatever-it-was, with a picture of a teddy bear on the front of it.

The K-Mart experience behind her, Katriana was ready to regain control of her situation. She thought she was doing quite well until . . .

"White meat or dark?" Ian asked.

She wasn't paying attention. Her mind was wandering. English wasn't her first language and something must have gone awry in her translation.

"I beg your pardon?"

"Chicken. White meat or dark?" he repeated.

"Chicken?"

"We're about to have chicken for lunch and I was trying to be polite."

Ian was *not* trying to be polite. Any imbecile could see that.

"I prefer *la cuisse*. Baked in white wine and garlic, I believe is the way our chef describes it on the daily menu."

"What the hell piece is that?" he growled.

"*La cuisse* is the piece above the long bone of the leg, here." She was even so helpful as to point to the corresponding part of her own anatomy. "The meat is juicy and flavorful."

"I guess I can get you a couple of thighs easy enough, Princess, but I doubt that white wine is anywhere in the Colonel's list of eleven secret herbs and spices. I wouldn't be surprised to find some garlic salt in there someplace, but forget the white wine. Besides, this chicken is gonna be fried. Not baked."

"Will we eat chicken *here?*" she asked, as he turned into the parking lot of a small white building and drove around toward the back.

"Smart lady," he mumbled, then rolled down his window and turned to speak into the gaudy menu display. "One two-piece thigh dinner and one two-piece breast dinner, with potatoes and slaw. And two iced teas."

"Slaw? What is slaw?"

"Cabbage and stuff. You'll like it. It's probably even good for you."

A disembodied voice crackled and instructed Ian to drive to the window, which he did. There he presented his money and, in exchange, was handed two boxes and two large covered cups.

"Our chicken is in these boxes?" she wondered, confused. The sauce would seep through the flimsy cardboard. Where was the cutlery? "I don't understand."

"You know what, Katie?" Ian said. She watched the muscles in his jaw flex, relax, then flex again as he pulled away from the window and parked. "I think you just hit the nail on the head. That's the root of all your problems. You just don't understand."

He opened one of the boxes and peered inside. "This one

91

is yours," he announced, and handed it to her.

The aroma was delectable, but what did one do with a box of chicken? How did one go about eating it? She stared at it and frowned.

"It's edible, Katie. You can pick it up and eat it."

"Pick it up? With my fingers?" She was mortified.

"Yeah. Pick it up. Like this." Ian demonstrated, then gnawed into his piece of chicken, as an animal would do.

"Oh, dear. One never . . ."

"Good God, Katie! Just pick up the freakin' chicken and bite into it." Ian was not a patient man, Katie realized. "Here."

He lifted a thigh from her box and held it for her.

"But . . ."

"But nothing. Take a bite. Now."

She nibbled.

He'd knitted his eyebrows—and she would have sworn he was quite angry with her but as soon as she bit into the chicken, Ian smiled. It wasn't a big smile, but it was enough to warm her insides. She wasn't sure she liked her insides that warm.

"It's quite good," she admitted.

He nodded, watching her as she finished chewing. After she indulged in another bite he attempted to place the chicken in her own hand but she shied away, unable to force herself to touch her food with her hands. One never did that, under any circumstances.

"This is just one more piece of Americana that you've got to get used to. Fast food."

"I am aware of fast food. I have even seen a McDonald's. I just haven't ever eaten from or in such . . . *establishments.*"

"Being aware of it and digging in and eating it are two different things. If we're being followed—and I'm not saying we are—but if we are, you'll stick out like a sore thumb eating your french fries and your fried chicken with a fork. We can disguise your face and your hair, but your eating habits will give you away for sure if you don't blend in with the rest of us heathens."

She laughed out loud at the idea of such a kind, if at times gruff, man identifying himself with heathens. "You are no heathen. Heathens wear animal skins and feathers and do evil fertility dances at midnight around campfires. They don't drive Porsches and rescue runaway royalty," she informed him. "And they would never do something so kind as to give midnight cups of cappuccino to frightened princesses who can't abide the taste of American coffee."

"You'd better stop now, Katie. You're making me sound like a nice guy. You'll ruin my image. And by the way, what's an evil fertility dance?"

"I have no idea." She swung her hair around a bit for effect and elevated her nose, feigning a haughtiness she no longer felt. "You insist that you're a heathen. You tell me."

He chuckled, warm and rich and low. Husky. Then he shook his head. "I'm not biting that one because I don't think you'd be too interested in my idea of a fertility dance."

Mon dieu, she was blushing again. What had possessed her to discuss such things with a man who was little more than a stranger? A man who would soon be . . . what? Not really her husband, but not really *not* her husband either. He would think her forward and ill-bred.

"I'm—" she started to apologize, but he stopped her short.

"No, not another word, Katie. And don't look at me like that with those big, sad eyes. I'm the one who should apologize. That was a little crude and there was no excuse for it." He offered a contrite smile. "Am I forgiven?"

"Oui," she murmured, although she had found nothing that needed forgiving. She was the one who had prompted the naughty allusions. So very, very unlike her. How strange was his man's effect on her?

He rooted around in his chicken box and came up with a napkin and cellophane-wrapped plastic cutlery.

"You may be onto something, not getting grease all over your hands. Mine sure are a mess."

"A true heathen would lick his fingers."

He laughed. Really laughed this time. No apologetic smile or polite chuckle. "How does such a proper little princess know so much about heathens?"

At that moment, unbidden, Monique and her teachings flitted across Katriana's mind. Perhaps it was her nearness to him. Perhaps it was something else entirely.

"You'd be surprised at all the things I know," she offered.

Napkin in hand, Ian scrubbed at his fingers and hands. "I'm not going there either, Princess. Let's just forget about fertility dances and punching each other's buttons. We could have a real good time if we let ourselves, but there's just not much point to that, is there?"

"Non."

Silence. Deafening, uncomfortable silence settled around them.

"So, are we through here?" Ian asked, breaking the awful silence. When she failed to answer, he went off in another direction entirely. "Katie, I'm sorry."

"There's no need for—"

"There is *every* need," he interrupted. "I've never been known for my charming manners, and I just—don't—know—how—to—act." He placed specific emphasis on each, separate word.

"You act very fine," she reassured him, then decided that

those words didn't sound right together. But her meaning was clear.

He dropped his head back against the headrest and closed his eyes. "I keep forgetting that you're a damned princess. And you're alone here and scared and you don't have anybody but me." He opened his eyes and smiled. "God, I thought *my* life sucked. I can't even imagine what yours must be like."

She shrugged.

"I'll try to behave. I really will. It's just that I've never met anyone like you before and it's thrown me a little off stride."

"Well, if it's any comfort, I've never met anyone like you either," she confessed.

He pondered that statement for a bit longer than she felt it deserved. Finally, he asked, "Is that a good thing or a bad thing?

She shrugged. "*Je n'sais pas.*"

"And that means . . . ?"

"It means I don't know."

It was the unfortunate truth.

Ian found two adjacent motel rooms and insisted that Katriana take a nap.

"You drove all night. Remember?"

She did remember, and was exhausted. Besides, the last few hours had been so full of new experiences and, yes, strange, unresolved feelings, if she were honest with herself. "I don't need a great amount of sleep," she murmured, genteel manners winning out even over her exhaustion.

"I'll just bet you don't," he muttered. "Late nights with the boys on the Riviera—that kind of thing?"

"What boys?"

He shot one eyebrow straight up in disbelief, followed by a

smile that wasn't a smile at all. It was something rather sad. He shook his head—unwilling, for some reason, to elaborate.

"Go on, now. Lay down. Take a nap. Later on we'll have some dinner and after that, if you behave yourself, I'll take you someplace that you'll love so much you might even decide to hug me before we're through."

Stinging from the "boys on the Riviera" remark, she froze him with a frosty glance. "I can't imagine anything you could possibly do that would encourage me to hug you."

"Don't be so quick to make rash statements, Princess," he cautioned. "After all, we're going to have to decide what to do about getting married before those Pinkerton guys find us again, and it just wouldn't be right for royalty such as yourself to get married in blue jeans from K-Mart. Soooooo . . . ," he dramatically stretched out the word, "I'm about to offer you two things that most women would sell their souls for."

Selling her soul was not on Katriana's current agenda, but she was determined to remain polite. "And those would be . . . ?"

"Those, my dear, would be my platinum credit card and a trip to the mall."

Somewhere between the nap and the mall, Ian decided that he wasn't cut out for intrigue. He couldn't shake the feeling that an entire battalion of Pinkerton detectives was hot on their heels, right around the corner, just out of sight.

And if that weren't bad enough, he and Katie had spent most of the afternoon cruising some of the most unsavory streets he'd ever seen.

Atlanta was a huge metropolitan center, as well as a major airline hub and international port of entry. He hadn't expected it to be as easy to purchase a new identity for Katie in Atlanta as he'd heard it was in Miami or New York, but it shouldn't have been as impossible as it was turning out to be. The crux of the problem seemed to be that he had no idea just where in Atlanta, or how, someone went about buying forged citizenship documents.

He wasn't so naïve as to expect to see signs in windows blatantly offering such a service. What he did expect—or more correctly, hope—was that if by some miracle he could find the right area of town where such things were available, he would realize that he was on the right track. He knew, of course, that Katie's new identity would cost him. Fortunately, money wasn't a problem. The problem lay in finding, and recognizing that he had found, the service itself.

Rumor had it that fake passports could be bought on almost any street corner in certain areas of certain cities. Unfortunately, he and Katie didn't happen to be in those particular cites. If a fake passport or Social Security card or even birth certificate could be found in Atlanta, he had every intention of tracking it down.

"Are we going to shop in *this* place?" Katie wondered, and he detected a hint of desperation in her tone. She must be in her mall mode. Probably because he had neglected to mention the nature of their current mission, which took priority over any trousseau shopping at the mall. Without the fake citizenship papers there would be no wedding. And with no wedding, no wedding finery would be necessary.

He didn't blame her for worrying about their current surroundings. He had some concerns of his own about this place. An abandoned old factory was the only building on the street they found themselves exploring, along with a profusion of litter whirling around in sporadic gusts of wind. The sun, shining bright and happy far above, seemed wary of allowing its light to penetrate the gloom surrounding them.

No human ventured to travel this street. Ian wished he hadn't either.

But he needed some sort of falsified proof of American citizenship for Katriana if they had any hope of getting married. The United States had strict laws concerning its marriage to non-citizens. He was more than willing to break every damned one of those laws, but he needed a little guidance in how to go about it.

"Why are we here?" Katriana whispered. She too felt that this godforsaken place oozed an almost tangible foulness.

Maybe it was time to explain things to her. A pampered, sheltered existence is a lovely life, until the realities of the world step in. This identity predicament was not his problem alone. In fact, it wasn't even *his* problem at all. It was *her* problem. But he sank deeper into it the farther he drove down streets like this on. He was prepared to offer bribes and purchase reams of illegal identity papers, if necessary.

And, God help him, if the press ever got wind of what he was up to, whatever tenuous hold he might still have on the pathetic dregs of his career would be gone forever. Any hint of misconduct was a death knell in the eyes of those sponsors who poured so many millions into his race team. His need to race again was as great as his need to draw his next breath, so why was he now putting himself in this precarious position? The simple answer was that he had no idea why, other than that Katie and her problems had wormed their way under his skin. If he didn't do everything in his power to save her from her father and his prospective seventy-nine-year-old son-in-law, Ian would never forgive himself.

Unfortunately, balancing the rigid requirements of his career against his newfound sense of duty seemed to result in an inane solution. He was a certified idiot to be chasing his own tail through the more unsavory parts of Atlanta, trying to buy forged citizenship papers for a freakin' princess, when he could be sitting on his Daytona Beach balcony, enjoying the ocean breeze, healing his damaged parts, and drowning his miseries in something tall and cold and mind-numbing.

Katie had asked why they were there, and she deserved an honest answer.

"Katie, what we're trying to do is find somebody who can sell us a forged United States passport. And I have to admit that it's not quite as easy as I thought it would be." He heaved a sigh.

"But why can we not use mine?" she asked.

Bless her sheltered little heart. And please, God, give him the patience to deal with her, when what he wanted to do was beat his head against the steering wheel.

Instead he tried logic. "You can't marry in the United States if you're not a United States citizen unless you have a special visa. It takes time to do that, and in your case, even if it was granted, there would be such a big to-do in the newspapers, your father couldn't miss it. So we've got to handle it this way."

"But Ian, please listen to me," she instructed. She had adopted the tone of someone speaking to a half-wit. "As I asked before, why can we not use my own passport?"

"Because it would prove that you aren't an American citizen." His patience was close to gone.

"But I *am* an American citizen and I entered the United States with a United States passport."

"That's impossible," he roared despite his good intentions. He simply couldn't help it. "You're a citizen of Île d'Arinedra. Hell, you're the damned princess of the place!"

"But I am also a United States citizen. My mother was from the United States and through her I am also a United

States citizen. I carry citizenship of both countries."

"No."

"Mais oui."

He shook his head. He had wasted the entire afternoon spinning his wheels, looking for someone who would take his money and show him how to commit a federal crime. All for the sake of marrying a woman he didn't want to marry and who didn't want to marry him.

He pulled the Porsche over to the curb and stopped. Perhaps it wasn't the wisest thing to do in this part of town, but if he hadn't, he might very well have rammed it straight into the nearest building.

"Why didn't you tell me this before?" he asked through his clenched teeth. It was a simple question. He wasn't yelling. He wasn't raving. He was asking a rational question.

And, by God, he wanted an answer!

Katriana's look overflowed with enough regal annoyance to fry a hamburger. She waited a beat or two, no doubt to confirm that her royal displeasure had been noted, then countered with an icy, "Why didn't you ask?"

She glared.

He glared back.

She won that particular stare-down when he blinked and looked away.

Did she never blink? Was that royal power instilled in her from birth? The ability to stare, unblinking, for hours and hours?

How infuriating! And useless!

"I guess we can get blood tests and a license," he offered through clenched teeth. "Assuming neither of us has any nasty diseases, we can be married by this time tomorrow."

"So soon?" She looked alarmed. Her princess persona evaporated in a flash.

"No waiting period in Georgia, Princess. I've already checked that out."

He watched a lone teardrop swell in the corner of her eye. She tried to blink it away, but he saw it and his righteous anger deflated like a two-day-old balloon.

"It's your call, Katie," he told her with surprising gentleness for a man who had been roaring with frustration seconds before. "All you have to do is say no and it's off. If you want out, just say so. No questions asked. Nobody owes anybody anything."

She smiled and—oh Lord—laid her soft, cool hand on his arm. Nothing more than that. Just a simple, friendly touch. The hairs on his arm stood straight up. He tried to breathe but couldn't manage much more than a ragged wheeze.

"You are wrong, Ian Grayson." She squeezed his arm just the barest bit and he almost groaned. "I owe you so very much. I can never repay you, but I will do what I can to try."

He didn't dare explore what she might mean.

Princess Katriana St. Ranganaux of Île d'Arinedra had, by right of her birth, expected a certain grandeur at her wedding. Although Ian purchased an exquisite silk suit in a lovely shade of ecru for her bridal dress, it was by no stretch of the imagination the bejeweled lace gown she had envisioned.

Ian, traveling with nothing more than a change or two of casual clothing, had outfitted himself in a dark charcoal-colored suit. Again, this was hardly the full ceremonial military dress uniform—complete with sash, medallions, and epaulettes—that Katriana had anticipated would adorn her groom, but she admitted that in his new suit and carefully knotted red and gray silk tie, Ian looked splendid.

The afternoon ceremony at the courthouse was composed

of little more than a question or two, which Ian had instructed her beforehand to answer in the affirmative.

No one made any inquiry about her identity. The American passport was, of course, in order. If anyone at the courthouse made the connection between the young European bride with the United States passport and the Runaway Princess, no one mentioned it.

In truth, Katriana suspected she could have been an ape and no one would have noticed. Everyone involved in the their brief civil ceremony was too busy asking for Ian's autograph to pay attention to his bride, whoever she might be. Perhaps he was indeed telling the truth when he told her he was a celebrity.

The ceremony ended with a perfunctory, no-nonsense kiss, in no way resembling Ian's previous kiss. This one was dry as powder. No more than a quick brush of his lips against hers and it was over, leaving her less than satisfied.

"Welcome to my world, Katie Grayson," he murmured into her hair at the end of that kiss, and for a brief, unguarded moment she could almost believe that he meant it. But of course, it was all for show.

So, what happens now? she wondered. Their wedding night was approaching. She realized that their marriage, which wasn't even a real marriage in the eyes of the Church, existed only for the sake of her protection. But Monique had been most explicit in her teachings about a man's expectations—*any* man's expectations. Ian had gone to such trouble to protect her. He could rave on and on about the differences between civil and religious marriages, and she understood those differences. Ian had done her a huge favor by marrying her. And even though she herself had established no consummation as one of her conditions for the marriage, she knew of only one way she might repay this man for his kindness. She possessed the necessary skills, although she had never put them to use.

There was also the added bonus that once the deed was done, she would no longer be the virgin bride her father had promised to Sir Christian. Even if the Church never sanctified her marriage to Ian, she would be forever relieved of the tiresome burden of her virginity. If it was necessary that she be deflowered—and it did, indeed, seem to be necessary—she wanted Ian to be the one. The problem was remaining emotionally uninvolved throughout the experience.

What a lot of balls to keep in the air all at one time!

"Maybe we ought to celebrate tonight and go dancing," Ian suggested as they walked back to his car.

"Dancing?"

"Yeah, dancing." Must he constantly aim that heart-stopping grin directly at her? "You any good at doing the two-step?"

"I have no idea," she confessed. She had never heard of the two-step. "But if it's some sort of local dance, I suspect I can master it. I have received quite rigorous dancing instruction since I was five years old."

"You ever danced in boots, Princess?" was his next cryptic question.

"Boots? Who dances in boots?"

"Katie Grayson, there's a whole world out there you have no idea even exists," he announced. "And by God, I've got a feeling that in addition to saving your elegant little butt from the clutches of that dirty old geezer, it's my duty to show you how the other half lives."

Had she married a lunatic? Ian's eyes danced with merriment. His dimples flashed. At that moment, he was the most handsome man she had ever known.

"And I have to learn all about this new world while trying

to dance in boots?" she asked.

"And a hat. You gotta have the right hat if you're gonna do the two-step."

"I can only imagine."

"No, sweetheart, I doubt that you can. I doubt that you have any idea what I'm talking about."

She bristled. *Sweetheart?*

Too familiar. Too affectionate. Simply too much to bear in her current emotional state.

"OK, here's the drill," Ian continued, unaware of her chaotic state. "We'll go back and change clothes, then I'm gonna find someplace to buy us each a pair of the flashiest damned boots around, as well as a couple of hats. After that, we'll top it all off with some hot dogs, so you can practice touching your food and licking your fingers, then we'll head for Cooter's and some beer and a little two-stepping. You think you can handle all that?"

"That doesn't sound too dreadful," she replied, hoping she sounded more courageous than she felt. Her new life was growing stranger with each passing hour.

Ian smiled and flashed his dimples at her. She wished he would quit doing that. No doubt he was a master in the art of flirting, and she had a woeful lack of experience in such arts. But, whether or not he was flirting, she owed him a tremendous debt for all he had done for her in the past few days. And now that he was her husband, she also owed him something else.

Perhaps this was as good a time as any to assure him that regardless of the circumstances of their union, she was willing to fulfill her duties as his wife.

"Ian," she began, struggling to find the correct words. "I am prepared to perform sexual acts."

Ian's car keys hit the ground. Ian himself came perilously

close to walking straight into a parked car. When he had recovered sufficiently, he turned on her as if she had just uttered blasphemy. She began to fear that, once again, perhaps she had not chosen the best words to convey her intention.

"God Almighty, woman!" he roared.

"I thought you would want to know."

"Well, now I know. I'll keep that in mind."

"There is no need to shout."

"Look, Princess, I'm trying to help you out here, but you're not cutting me any slack at all. Let's just keep our eyes on the ball and focus on losing those detectives. Okay? We don't even know each other very well. I'm no prude, but I see no point in jumping into bed together just because one of us got a little horny. Are you with me so far?"

He must have taken her silence as an affirmative response because he continued. "I've been down that road and, believe me, it leads nowhere. It'll just confuse the issue and make things much more difficult. So let's just shake hands right here and now and agree to stay out of each other's pants."

"I merely assumed that you would want to receive what is rightfully yours."

"And that would be . . . what?" He then answered his own question. "Those sexual acts you're prepared to perform?" He snorted—*the man actually snorted like a swine!* "Yesterday when I tried to kiss you, you wouldn't even open your mouth. And now you're prepared to *perform sexual acts?*"

"There is no need to be rude."

"And there is no need for *you* to proposition me right here in the middle of the street."

"I did *not* proposition you!"

"Well, what do you call it?"

"I offered my sexual skills to my husband."

105

"And your husband has declined."

"But men always want—" she started to tell him of what Monique had assured her was true of all men, but then reconsidered.

"And this one is no different, but we just won't go there. Okay?" He looked out of sorts—no outrageous grin, no nothing . . . except for an angry scowl.

"Très bien," she agreed, cool and haughty. At least that was how she struggled to appear. But it was possible that her shaking hands and stiff, clumsy legs had given her away.

Ian Grayson was a difficult man to decipher. Up until that moment he had been friendly, easy to be with, willing to help her—and, hardest of all for her to accept, trustworthy. Trust was something she did not bestow lightly. Her trusted father had bartered her to an old man, which had inclined her against bestowing trust on anyone ever again.

But she had violated her most basic instinct, let down her guard and trusted Ian Grayson, a stranger. And as a token of that trust, she had offered him her body.

Although she was much too embarrassed to state it explicitly, a man of honor would realize that her virginity was an important part of that offer. Yet Ian had declined with a brusqueness that was confusing and insulting.

I should be relieved, she thought. The very notion of performing those sexual acts with a real man, with Ian Grayson, was humiliating. So why this sudden disappointment? Why was she on the verge of tears? Monique had warned her that there would be little pleasure in it for her, but for a crazy minute Katriana had been besieged by strange, unsolicited visions of Ian's hands learning the contours of her body . . . his mouth tasting her breasts . . . his body filling her . . . finding its explosive release deep inside of her.

Of course, Monique had also instructed her that if she did

her job correctly, there would be no need for actual penetration. Monique was of the opinion that the act of penetration would be difficult for Sir Christian because of his age, so she had taught Katriana how to please him in other ways. She had even suggested that Katriana, and probably Sir Christian as well, would prefer it that way.

Ian was still glowering as he deposited her into the passenger seat and then slid in behind the wheel. His movements as he started the car were jerky, almost uncoordinated.

"I'm sorry. I didn't mean to be rude about it, but I just . . ." He faltered and searched for a way to complete his thought. His next word gave Katriana an entirely new perspective on their conversation.

". . . can't . . ."

He continued and said more, but she ignored the rest of it. Her focus rested on that one word, *can't.*

His wreck, she realized with dismay. *Poor Ian can't perform because of his injuries!*

Perhaps her training could be of some use to this man. She'd already decided that Ian would be the one to take her virginity. If Ian did in fact possess . . . difficulties . . . then with her training she was the perfect person to assist him. And he must overcome those difficulties before he could perform his duty.

Certainly, if she could overcome impotence in an old man, she could do the same with a younger one. Couldn't she? After all, impotence was impotence, whatever the age. Right?

There was only one way to find out.

"I'm sorry. I didn't mean to be rude about it, but I just . . . can't . . . let that happen between us right now," he tried to explain.

Katriana looked as if he had kicked her in the stomach. He

knew that feeling very well. He had experienced it himself when she announced, right in the middle of the damned parking lot, that she was *prepared to perform sexual acts.*

That was *not* a smart thing to tell a guy who had spent the entire day and most of the long night before fighting his physical urges. A guy whose hormones were screaming that he take her up on her offer, escort her back to the motel posthaste and let her perform any sexual act her little heart desired, as long as she was quick about it.

He didn't say any of that, of course. But God, he was tempted! This woman—this royal princess from some Mediterranean island kingdom off the coast of France—had kindled a fire in his belly . . . and lower. He was consumed with feelings for her he neither wanted nor could handle. He didn't dare touch her. When he had risked kissing her at that pitiful excuse for a wedding, it had taken all his willpower to keep it quick and clean.

When she propositioned him, his first heady reactions were, *Why the hell not? Who can it hurt? I'm not European royalty, but I'm not gutter trash either. She's as hot for me as I am for her.*

But he couldn't do that to her, or to himself. He hadn't felt love in ages, not since Cheryl, but he was currently experiencing a sensation like love, and he didn't like anything about it. They were so very wrong for each other. Better to keep the pseudo marriage simple. He would have to nurse himself through enough hurt when it was over, without the added complications that accompanied the sex.

So why was she now smiling? He decided to ask her.

"Why are you smiling?"

"I am so very sorry. I know it's not a funny thing, but I just . . ." Her voice trailed off and he never did learn what the reason for her smile. She sat beside him with the demeanor of someone reviewing a mental checklist. Every so often she would nod, then squint her eyes as if deep in thought. Then another nod. Odd behavior, to say the least.

"We don't have to go to Cooter's, if you don't want to," he offered. He hoped to hell she wouldn't accept. He needed to be away—*far away*—from those motel rooms this evening. He possessed a reasonable amount of willpower, but not enough to resist this enchanting woman if she had sex on her mind.

"Oh, I'm looking forward to it," she responded with genuine enthusiasm.

"I doubt that."

"And may I ask why you would doubt that?"

"Just because," he grunted. She eyed him suspiciously. "Because you have no idea where you're going or what you're going to do when you get there."

"It's nothing awful, is it?"

"No, it's nothing awful. But it'll be something new to you, something I'm sure you've never done before."

"Well, perhaps it's time for me to learn some new things."

"You're pretty damned agreeable for a woman." He meant to tease her, but it came out sounding like he was grumbling. Probably because he was.

"Ah, Ian Grayson," she answered, and he could discern a *tut-tut* in her voice. Then she smiled. "You have no idea just how very agreeable I can be."

Standing close beside him in Cooter's, she was feisty as a colt in spring, her face slightly damp from constant dancing, her elegant hair hanging down her back in a single loose braid that he'd helped her style. It was the first attempt at a braid for either of them, but it had turned out pretty damned spectacular. At least he thought so.

The way she looked, her name really could be Katie Grayson.

Certainly in her new hat and boots, all dressed up in the calf-length, full denim skirt and peasant blouse he'd bought for her—Ian was a sucker for a woman in a denim skirt and a peasant blouse—she looked nothing at all like Princess Katriana Saint-whatever-her-name-was.

Ian took another long pull on his beer. Katie did the same, mimicking his movements. He had to admit she was a quick study.

And she wasn't wearing a bra.

That was the first thing that grabbed his attention when she floated out of her motel room, smelling like Sunday morning sin and dressed to kill in her brand-new Western finery, ready to take Cooter's by storm. He didn't know whether to make an issue out of her lack of appropriate support or to step quietly back inside his own room and try to find a bigger pair of jeans, because the jeans he wore had grown uncomfortably snug in the crotch. He hoped that she was wearing at least *some* kind of underwear, because if she wasn't, and he found out about it . . .

"Do you think anybody there might recognize me in these clothes?" she'd wondered.

"Honey, I don't even recognize you and I know who you are."

And that's the way the evening progressed. He would say something innocent and she would answer with something equally innocent. Then she would smile at him, or touch him, or do nothing more than look up at him, and he was ready to howl at the moon.

He spent a while teaching her to line dance, and the lady took to it as if she had been born to do it.

He demonstrated his theory on the proper way to drink

beer from a longneck bottle, holding the neck rather than the base, so as not to warm the beer with the heat from his hand.

Then she laughed her marvelous, tinkling laugh, and shared something with him about white wine and the preferred method of holding crystal stemware. He couldn't focus on exactly what she said with his blood roaring.

He led her through the paces of a fast two-step, swings and fancy steps included, and she followed his lead easily. Never missed a step.

He welcomed the exertion, even the pain in his leg, from all the dancing, because it served to divert his thoughts away from this beautiful woman who was driving him batty.

He could diagnose his problem but was at a loss to cure it. For the moment, he had no more brains or willpower than a lump of mush. But he was holding on . . .

. . . until the music changed, the lights lowered, and the band began a slow dance.

"You ready to sit one out?" he asked.

"No."

"You're not tired?"

"No."

So what were his choices? Stomp off the floor in a snit? Or gather her in his arms and damn the consequences?

He had to handle her very, very carefully because there was only one way he could hold her—and any number of ways he didn't dare to. Most of his pertinent parts had cooperated admirably and spent the evening settled into something approximating parade rest, but he was full of beer and his resistance was fading. He knew the minute he started touching her, holding her close to him, smelling her bewitching scent, he was a goner.

She moved in close to him at the same time he was trying to hold her out and away. To his dismay, he found that the tried and true method of holding a woman while slow dancing felt awkward, and not at all right for this particular dance and this particular woman. So, fool that he was, he dropped her hand and wound his arms around her.

They were doing precious little actual dancing, he realized, but there wasn't much he could do about that. His various body parts were refusing to obey any of the frantic instructions his brain was trying to issue.

He had believed that any couple taking up space on the dance floor ought to do the rest of the people in the room the courtesy of actually dancing. But for the moment, he couldn't manage much more than rocking back and forth with Katriana.

Hell, forget *Katriana*. Tonight, in her boots and her denim, and forever after in his mind and in his heart, she would be *Katie. His* Katie.

Other couples, serious about dancing a slow two-step, circled around them in an attempt to dodge the two rule-breakers. Ian didn't care a whit. Before this godforsaken night, he'd scoffed at men who kissed their partners on the dance floor, but he now found himself close to kissing Katie.

His befuddled brain demanded fresh air, space. He needed to be *away* from her. He needed to quit touching her. He needed a cigarette, something more potent than a beer, and a lonesome stroll in the frigid night air. Too bad he didn't smoke, couldn't stomach hard liquor with beer, and would find precious little frigid night air during August in Atlanta.

Besides that, he didn't dare leave her alone. So far, there was no indication that they were being followed, but he couldn't take the chance.

"Come on," he muttered, then turned her around and hustled her toward the door.

"Where are we going?"

"Outside."

"Why?"

"Because."

"I don't understand."

"Nobody said you had to understand."

"But—"

"We're just gonna step outside for a few minutes, to get some fresh air. To walk around a bit . . ."

He banged the front door open and piloted her through it, like a tugboat pushing a barge.

". . . in the rain," he finished, as they were greeted with a barrage of hot, sharp summer rain pellets. The still-hot tarmac steamed as the raindrops pounded it. Ian wouldn't have been surprised to find steam rising from where the drops landed on him. He was burning hot all over—everywhere, outside and in.

Sometimes, he thought, *God can make it very clear that He isn't on my side.*

"It's raining, Ian."

Didn't Katie realize that he knew this?

"Yeah," he grunted.

"It's raining *hard.*"

"Yeah."

"Why are we standing out here in the rain?"

"For God's sake, woman," he barked at her, for no real reason. The lady had done nothing except be her sweet, enchanting self. He was the one with the problem, and the warm summer rain wasn't cooling him off. It was only making him mad.

"Come on, girl. Run," he instructed.

He needed air and space. What he got was a mad dash to

his car through the pouring rain.

"Are we leaving?"

"I don't know," he grunted. "But right now, we're gonna get in the car. That's all I know."

"Are you okay?" she called over her shoulder through the downpour, as they dashed across the parking lot.

She sure is a speedy little thing, he noted, captivated by the swish of her denim skirt back and forth across her backside as she dashed across the parking lot.

"I'm fine," he yelled back at her through the pounding rain, "just great." But that wasn't the truth. "Here, get in the car."

He slammed the door shut behind her, then sprinted around to the other side and slid in behind the wheel.

Now what? he wondered, and cursed himself for not staying in Cooter's, where it was dry and where plenty of beer was available to dull his senses.

As for Katie, she seemed to be indulging herself in a veritable cuss-fest. He caught more than one *merde* sprinkled through her mutterings. Even he recognized the French equivalent of shit, confirming that Miss Perfect Princess could work up a serious potty mouth when the situation called for it.

That was very interesting, because until that very moment, Katie had exuded grace and manners.

But suddenly there seemed to be quite a lot upsetting her, the most aggravating being something to do with her hat. *Mon chapeau joli* meant *my pretty hat,* didn't it? She didn't much like her *chapeau joli* being so *très humide,* or so she grumbled as she shook the rain from her hat, and all over the car and him.

"Quit that," he said.

"Excusez-moi," she said . . . or asked . . . or something . . .

114

with a haughty glare down her regal nose. Of course, for that to happen she had to tilt her nose upward so she could see him. For some reason, he found the gesture captivating. His hormones, poised on the edge of madness, went berserk.

"Katie, stop it," he said—well, *begged* would be a better word. In the close quarters of the car, with the night wrapped around them, her mutterings, her scent, every damned thing about this woman, was making him crazy. He had to touch her. He had to kiss her.

"God, Katie, I . . ." he murmured, and then he gave up. He was through fighting it. His wild attraction to her was foolish, bordering on dangerous, but it was a fact, and by God, if he didn't kiss her, he thought he'd probably just explode.

He ached for her to open her mouth for him this time, but he couldn't form the words to communicate his need. His mouth was too busy kissing her to do much of anything else.

But he found there was no need for instruction. Her lips parted willingly. Her tongue met his, twined with it, welcomed it, then led it on a merry chase that drove him insane before it was over. He wanted to devour her. He had no real perception of what was happening, except that whatever it was, it was pure bliss.

The windows fogged over, from the heady burst of his own body heat, no doubt. As he noted the foggy curtain enveloping them, he swore under his breath at the Porsche's lack of functional space, limiting the progress of that momentous kiss. He had needs, dammit! Pounding, aching needs, daring him to act the part of a randy, besotted sixteen-year-old and make love to her right there in the cramped car. Needs that would drive him stark raving mad if they weren't met very soon.

Katie wasn't a venturesome kisser, but she followed his

115

lead. He slipped his hand down the front of her loose peasant blouse and found her luscious, unencumbered breasts. As he worked them free from her blouse, she breathed a long, contented sigh that convinced him she wasn't as indifferent to him as she pretended. At his touch, her nipples hardened into tight, tiny beads. He inched his greedy lips deliberately down along the slim column of her throat and across her chest, to flick his tongue over her left nipple, savoring each delectable inch of the journey. She tasted like she smelled, like flowers and spring. He took his time relishing that wonderful breast, then moved on to the right one, budded and ready for his attention. His tongue circled the taut nipple and . . .

Lightning shot straight through him!

Was he dreaming? Had he gone into such sexual overload that he was hallucinating?

Was Katie unzipping his jeans? Slipping her warm hand inside, touching him, stroking him?

He tensed, gritting his teeth. He didn't dare breathe. "No," he rasped, his mouth so rigid it could barely form the word. He knew he should push her hand, and the rest of her, away. But he could only thrust his aching, needy self into that hand, move with her rhythm, and reach for the release his body craved.

"Shhhh," she whispered, "Everything is fine. Let me help you. You can do this, Ian. I know you can."

Help you? What the hell did she mean? She was helping him all right. Helping him make a damn fool of himself. Helping him hurl himself over the edge of the world into a blazing, beckoning abyss that was either love or hell—probably both, if his prior experience with love were any indication.

Help me do what? he wondered, then heard himself ask it out loud, somewhere between one of those humiliating groans and the next.

"Oh, Ian, you hardly have any problem at all. You are doing so very excellent. You really are. I think you're going to . . . very, very soon."

What the hell did that mean?

The whole focus of his being was centered just below his belt, wrapped in that silken hand that was stroking him to distraction and his ears weren't registering sounds correctly. The *very, very soon* part did, however, register, and it was the gospel truth.

"I can't . . ." he began, trying to tell her that his time was up. He couldn't hold himself back much longer. He needed for her to stop—then—*that very second*—but, if she *did* stop, he might die on the spot. "Katie, please—"

"But of course you can, Ian. You truly can. I know you can."

"Please don't—" he tried one last, pitiful time, his voice husky and thick.

"I won't stop," she whispered. "I promise."

It sounded like a sacred vow.

He was sweating blood to hold himself back, and she was doing everything in her power to make it happen.

God help him. Time was up. Flickering tongues of flame danced up the insides of his thighs then billowed and engulfed him. He stiffened and tried to choke back the groan he felt welling up through layers of sensation. With a rush of intense pleasure, and a simultaneous rush of embarrassment, he gave up.

Whatever obscure, incomprehensible game Katie was playing, she had finally won.

Chapter 7

Atlanta was stifling hot, and marriage to Ian—even a few days of it—was not what Katriana had expected.

Nothing about it was right. Nothing.

Ian would barely speak to her. More than that, he refused to make eye contact. Their former camaraderie had disappeared, and he sulked around in a state of constant embarrassment.

But why?

Monique's teachings had been quite specific concerning a man's sexual needs, and his satisfaction was perhaps the most treasured event in his life. Even an old man like Sir Christian would thank her for bestowing such a gift on him. One might assume that Ian would be thrilled and delighted to find that sexual function was still a possibility for him.

But Ian's behavior was nothing like what Monique had led her to expect.

Besides his less-than-thrilled reaction to his remarkable recovery from impotence, there was the puzzle of his . . . well, to be quite blunt, his male organ. Monique was very knowledgeable about male anatomy and wonderfully patient with her pupil. But Monique's lessons had left a bit to be desired.

Having no actual man on whom to practice, during their sessions Katriana had been instructed only verbally about that particular organ, where to find it, how to identify it by touch, how it would react to various stimuli, and so on.

But Ian Grayson fit none of the criteria Monique had taken pains to teach to her, and the inconsistencies of his own male organ with Monique's teachings puzzled her. Monique, of course, had taught Katriana with Sir Christian, not Ian Grayson, in mind. But could one human male be so different from another?

Katriana blamed her own inexperience with men for her confusion. Certainly it wasn't her teacher's oversight. Monique was knowledgeable about Sir Christian and many, many other men his age, as she had been quick to inform Katriana before they began any training exercises. Monique's specialty seemed to be men of advanced years.

And now Ian was upset. She had been unfailing in her attempts to do everything in their daily life as correctly as possible, even to the point of keeping her motel room neat and tidy the way he liked it, in the hope that he might drop in from next-door to visit . . . or watch television . . . or even something else. She refused to name precisely what she wished he would drop by to do. His potency appeared to have been restored, she was his lawful wife, and she was indeed curious about the secrets between husbands and wives.

Monique had cautioned her that she herself would experience precious little physical pleasure from the act. But when he wasn't sulking, Ian was a kind and generous man, as well as a clever one. She rather doubted that Sir Christian would have the energy or the inclination to see to her pleasure, but with Ian, she had expected more.

But no. She had been married to him for close to a week and was still as virginal and untouched as the day she married him. In the end, perhaps that would be best, because she was developing strong feelings for him, feelings that left her vulnerable to his dark moods and his lack of interest in her. He had shown not the slightest inclination to repeat their sexual encounter, although she was convinced that he had enjoyed it.

She sighed and once again picked up the magazine she'd tossed aside. Was this to be her life? Frittering away her time in one room while in the other Ian talked nonstop on the telephone to some man named Benny about engines and spoiler angles and tire pressures and what someone might care to do "in the center of the corner to gain a tenth or two," whatever that meant.

But according to Ian, after today any frittering away that she did would occur in another room, in another town. A place she had never heard of in her life. Somewhere in South Carolina—wherever South Carolina might be. A place called Darlington.

And, as if traveling to the wilds of Darlington, South Carolina were't bad enough, Ian babbled that his motor coach would be waiting there for them.

Wasn't that some sort of a bus?

She sighed with frustration.

At the moment, it was her peculiar lot to be married to a semi-retired racecar driver who was still healing from horrible injuries. She had helped him achieve an almost miraculous recovery from impotence, but he still wanted nothing at all to do with her. And that wasn't the worst of it.

From what little she could comprehend of his conversations with this Benny person, and the very few things he shared when he deigned to speak to her, whenever they arrived in Darlington *they would be living on a bus!*

Ian found the galloping mess that he called his life almost funny. If he hadn't been so humiliated, he might have been able to laugh about it. But he was far too embarrassed to allow any humor or enjoyment creep into anything involving Katie.

"You live in a bus?" she screeched when he explained where they were headed.

"Sometimes," he replied, amazed at how much defensiveness he could pour into that one word.

What the hell was wrong with a customized bus that cost the better part of a million dollars? He was a racecar driver, for God's sake. He couldn't weave his way at six o'clock every morning through throngs of adoring fans to get from a motel to the racetrack. During race season, drivers lived their lives in a community of luxury buses and campers that accompanied them from track to track. The new and temporary Mrs. Grayson would have to tolerate it. End of explanation.

"Mon dieu," she snorted under her breath. Her Royal Highness wasn't the slightest bit enamored about the prospect of living on a bus.

She was happier—but only slightly—when she saw the bus Friday morning as they drove into Darlington Raceway's drivers' compound.

"It's not *awful*," she conceded with a pretty little pout.

"Not awful? It's expensive as hell!" he exclaimed.

"I expected, perhaps, a double-decker, or a child's bus, or—"

"What in the hell is a *child's bus?*"

"Such as children ride to school here in your country."

"You thought I'd make you camp out in a school bus?"

"I had no idea what you meant when you said we would sleep in your bus." Her royal back stiffened, emphasizing her point even further. "I am unaccustomed to any form of wilderness survival."

Wilderness survival?

That hurt. Almost as much as realizing that she thought he would stick her in nasty, run-down school bus. She probably imagined herself stranded in a rusted-out, abandoned derelict, set up on blocks, overgrown with weeds.

What kind of man did she think he was?

"Katie, I'm not a caveman. I do have a little class."

"It is possible that I overreacted," she conceded. "This is actually quite adequate."

Ian smiled. He probably shouldn't have. But for the moment he ignored the ever-present, black cloud of humiliation that hung over his head, and he relaxed and allowed himself to smile. Poor Katie was making such a valiant effort to adapt to a culture as alien to her as a colony of Martians.

She smiled back at him—and oh, God, he wished she hadn't. It was an adorable, captivating burst of a smile that could have charmed the pants right off him. But he refused to let himself get caught in her trap again. She was full of wiles and tricks, and he was fresh out of defenses. Besides that, he had work to do.

"It's bigger inside than it looks. I think you'll be comfortable here because—"

She wasn't listening to a word he said. She had already put her doubts behind her. As soon as he unlocked the door, she scampered up the steps into her new, temporary, home. Watching her whirl around and around, awestruck and delighted at the same time, he ached with longing for things that had no place in his life, impossible things.

"I think I like it," she announced.

"Well, that's just dandy," he grunted. If a simple smile from her could launch him like the space shuttle, he'd do well to remain grumpy and unapproachable.

It was probably just as well, because even now, after obsessing for days about those few memorable moments they had shared, he still couldn't pinpoint the word to define that bittersweet combination of thrill and humiliation.

"A table and a television and—oh, look!—*une petite*

cuisinière!" She spun around again, her excitement growing by the moment, over something as simple as a damned drop-in stove. "I will learn to cook for you, Ian," she vowed. "I swear it. I promise I will."

"Well, let's not go overboard," he cautioned. He had serious doubts that Katie had ever been in the same room with a stove until the night they'd met, when she'd killed that potato. He also had serious doubts that his digestive tract was prepared for her culinary talents.

"Are there not books that describe how to do such things?"

"Well, I believe there are, but—"

"So?" She shrugged her charming shrug and chased it with the innocent smile that never failed to rock his world.

His gaze skimmed over her. He couldn't drag it away, and he wished he'd possessed enough sense that day at K-Mart not to buy her those cute knit shirts with their itty-bitty, thin straps across the delicate span of her tanned shoulders. His educated guess as to the "medium" size had been right on the money, but those shirts fit a little too well.

". . . if you would do that, I would so very much appreciate it," she finished yet another of her rambling, confusing, dissertations. Too bad, he'd missed everything after the *so* and the shrug, but in an effort to appear at least marginally rational, he nodded and agreed . . .

. . . which incurred a hopeful look and her open palm extended toward him. It also engendered confusion on his part as to what he might have just agreed to.

"I cannot find a market in your car without the keys, can I?"

She looked delicious enough to bite, and he might have sold his soul for the chance to do that.

But drive his car?

That was something else entirely. In his exhaustion during the midnight drive from Daytona Beach to Atlanta, he'd wavered, and she hadn't done a half-bad job of it. But this was a little different. He wouldn't be there if she ran into problems. Got lost.

Never came back.

"And some money. I will need some money to buy the book to tell me how to cook," she declared, "and, of course, some food."

"The racecar is being unloaded now, Katie. I've gotta get over there. We'll talk about this later. Okay?" he waffled and tried to scoot out the door.

"What racecar?" she asked, one eyebrow creeping up in disbelief, the other lowering over her eye in rebuke. "Who is unloading what racecar?"

"My racecar," he answered quickly and moved toward the door. But he wasn't quick enough.

"Why must you be there?"

He wanted to believe that the worry he saw lurking in her eyes was real. That maybe she cared about what happened to him. But she'd delivered herself into his hands for safe-keeping, and if he messed up and wrecked again, she would be once again on her own. Her worry was for herself, certainly not for him. But for just the briefest tick, when he first saw it, his heart had soared.

"Because I'm the driver," he answered evenly, "and I've gotta *drive*." It was becoming imperative that he escape. Despite her underlying motives, she looked too much like a wife, reprimanding him with her eyes for not having bothered to mention the fact that he intended to strap his not-yet-healed self inside a racecar and hurtle it around the Darlington Raceway at more than 150 miles per hour.

"You are not yet able to drive. You cannot even walk properly," she informed him, as if he didn't know.

"I'll be okay. It's a car race, not a footrace." His feeble attempt at humor went unnoticed.

"You said someone else now drove your car. What about him? Where is this person? Why is *he* not driving the car? Why must you?"

He spied a couple of tears lurking at the corners of her eyes, trying to decide whether to take the plunge down her cheeks or stay where they were and shimmer until they drove him crazy.

"Katie, calm down. And, for God's sake, please, *please* don't cry," he begged.

She looked away. "I am very sorry. I will not."

She crossed her elegant arms and hugged her body as if seeking comfort from the only available source, her own self.

And that hurt him—more than he cared to put into words. Why couldn't she trust *him* to comfort her, look to *him* to touch her and hold her if she needed to be held?

Why indeed! To her he was little more than a stranger. A helpful one, perhaps, but still an unknown quantity.

A commoner.

"Katie, it's okay. In fact, I'm touched you would care whether I tried to drive again or not." *Merciful heaven that was hard to say.*

"I don't think you're ready, Ian. I saw your wreck. I saw how horrible it was." She lost her fight with the tears and the first two slipped down her cheeks, with two more welling up behind them. "Where is this man who drove in your place?"

"He's sick, in the hospital."

"*Mon dieu!* Did he wreck also?" She looked almost frantic.

"No, sweetheart, he didn't wreck," he replied, wondering where the hell the *sweetheart* had come from. "He had his appendix removed yesterday and he can't race for a while.

125

I'm just filling in for my fill-in." He might have laughed at the absurdity of the situation, but he saw her quiver, then start shaking, huddled in her own arms.

"You don't have to worry. I'll be fine," he assured her, then wished that someone could assure him of that same thing.

"But aren't you afraid?" she inquired. "Aren't you afraid to get back in that car and drive so fast?"

He acknowledged her concern by considering his answer before he gave it, instead of pooh-poohing her worry for him, a man who should have meant nothing at all to her. She was a stranger, after all, who had dropped into his life for a short time. He had no claim on her affections or anything else. There was no real reason for her concern—if it was genuine. But for that moment, it warmed him as nothing else had for a long time.

"I don't know how to do anything else," he admitted, almost in a whisper. It was a painful confession, and only then did he realize how true it was. "I've raced in one way or another since I've been old enough to drive. I guess the truth is that I'm afraid *not* to race."

"But you could die. Do you not realize that you might get in that car and never get out alive?"

"Oh, I realize it. I *always* realize it," he answered. "But I don't let it rule every move I make. I can't."

"Then you are either a very brave man or a very foolish one. I do not know you well enough to realize which one." Her gaze locked with his. Another couple of tears worked their way free and followed the others, unchecked.

"I've never considered myself either brave or foolish."

She didn't respond. She shook her head and glanced up at him, her eyes still brimming with tears.

"I've really got to go. The crew is waiting for me." He

jumped down the coach steps to the ground, escaping as fast as he could.

Then he remembered.

"Oh yeah," he said and spun back toward her. "Here're the car keys and some money." He tossed her the keys and a fistful of whatever bills he pulled from the stash of money in his pocket, which he'd brought from Florida. The bank withdrawal was mostly large bills. He was alarmed to see himself hand her at least two hundreds, two twenties and a fifty. The rest of the substantial wad was, no doubt, some further combination of those. The damned woman had turned him into an idiot, tossing money around and letting her run off with his beloved car. "Be careful. Don't get lost. And *be sure* to wear a hat and my sunglasses. I don't think anybody followed us, but I won't be with you, so be *very* careful. Okay?"

"*Oui,*" she agreed. She still looked sad, and so beautiful that he wondered how he could pull himself away from her, even to practice for the race. In a different time, with other women, he hadn't always been so chivalrous.

And what a strange commentary on his life that was! At one time he had loved Cheryl, the woman he'd married. Yet it was always easy to leave her, and impossible to leave those women who sought him out on the road, the ones whose names and faces were blurred and lost by the next morning.

Now he had another wife, and a relationship with her so convoluted that nobody, including Ian himself, could understand it. What he felt for her was so much like what he'd felt for Cheryl. But that had been love. This wasn't love. Or was it?

What he felt for Katie was also rife with those thundering hormonal meltdowns that overtook him periodically when he met some woman and knew in his gut that the chemistry was right . . . that the sex would be phenomenal. A guy wasn't supposed to feel that way about his wife.

So much uncertainty, all tangled up with his fiery attraction to Katie, created complications he didn't have the strength to unsnarl at this juncture in his life. He needed crisp, clear, clean-cut emotions. Not deep-shrouded feelings that clamored to be explored and dissected.

Too bad Katie wasn't just some bimbo. Because then he could toss her on the couch, give her what was pounding away for her inside his jeans, and in ten minutes he'd be on his merry way, with both of them grinning like pigs in mud.

But not Katriana. Not Katie. For all her apparent experience and skill, both of which she'd heaped on him a few nights ago, she had an air of naiveté, that drove him crazy.

"I should be back around six o'clock or so. And . . ." He didn't want to sound like a sap, but he had to make sure she understood, ". . . be careful. Be *really* careful. These people don't play games, and if they find you, they'll . . ." He couldn't find words to express his fear without frightening her, so he quit there.

This excursion into the wide world all alone, on her own, seemed important to her, so did he dare toss a wet blanket on it? Sometimes she cringed like a scared little rabbit, but once in a while—like now—her spunk came peeking through like the sun through a bank of rain clouds. How could a bird learn to fly if it never tested its wings?

"I know," she murmured. "I know." Then, "And you, Ian, you be very careful yourself. I would—" Katie stopped speaking exactly as he had done, also unable to find the right words. He wished he knew if it was the language barrier or an emotional barrier she was trying to find her way across. "I would miss you, Ian Grayson," she finished.

He stared back and said nothing as his heart overflowing with all those confounded feelings he didn't want to deal with. Didn't want to let into any part of his life.

He was afraid that his heart showed plainly in his eyes. Finally he forced himself to mumble, "I'll see you tonight," before he got himself in trouble; then he turned around and walked away. Through the village of motor coaches, toward the garage area, in the sweltering, South Carolina Labor Day weekend heat, he trudged.

He couldn't whistle. Never had been able to. But the song whirling around inside his head almost demanded to be whistled. It was catchy and he liked it . . .

. . . until he remembered the name of it.

"You Always Hurt the One You Love."

No, indeed! Ian resigned himself to the sad fact that he wasn't healed yet—not even close—and he had to wonder if he ever would be.

He returned to his motor coach hours later, exhausted, his leg, back, and head throbbing, and hungry as a bear. He had no expectation that Katie had done something so mundane as shop for groceries. In fact, he was primed to root around in the refrigerator, hoping that his coach driver had stocked it with something edible. Sometimes he did that for Ian. Sometimes he forgot.

But when he opened the door he was greeted with the succulent aroma of chicken. Nothing burnt—or raw—about it, so Katie couldn't have been involved.

Ian followed his nose up the three steps into the compact kitchen of the coach, his mouth watering—stomach growling.

He found flowers on the table. He found two places set with placemats and wine glasses.

He also found containers in the trash can that tattled of Katriana's discovery of a deli with precooked food. He said a quick thanksgiving to the Lord for leading her to the place, and smiled his first real smile in hours.

He found Katriana herself decked out in something new and silky—and probably expensive if he could judge such things. For damned sure, it wasn't anything he'd bought for her at K-Mart.

It wrapped around her elegantly, kind of like a sari. Just watching her move around in it, especially from the back, made Ian grind his teeth so hard they hurt.

Also relevant to his condition was that as closely as he looked for a hint of pantylines under that luscious concoction she wore, he found none whatsoever. He wished she'd just turn her pantyless bottom away from him—but when she did, he got an eyeful of two perky little nipples pressing against the front of her garb, and he prayed again for the pantyless bottom. The hint of nothing was far preferable to the presence of those tight, perfect, delectable buds right there before his eyes, pointing straight at him, daring him to lower his mouth to them . . . taste them . . .

He clamped his teeth shut to stifle a groan.

"Don't you think it's cold in here?" he growled.

"Non."

Besides having no panties and a couple of world-class nipples, she smelled heavenly. Ian wanted to settle in and take alternate bites of the chicken and of her.

"Everything looks lovely," he stammered, determined to keep the growl out of his voice.

Katie smiled. "You need not be concerned. It is all quite safe. I found a market that offers cooked food for sale. I feel perhaps enough confidence now to prepare an edible potato, but chicken . . ." She stopped and shrugged, then laughed. It tinkled like the vibration of crystal angel wings.

Predictably, Ian's body clenched, but somehow he managed not to grab her. He even smiled back at her. He could work up a killer smile when the need arose, and the need had definitely arisen.

"I'm starved," he offered in the name of polite conversation.

"*Bien,*" she answered, leaving Ian to wonder why it should be good that he was starved. Unless Katie was beginning to feel domestic.

She opened the refrigerator door and disappeared behind it, only to reappear seconds later with a bottle of wine. He didn't recognize the bottle, or the label, and assumed that it had probably cost him dearly if it was something she was accustomed to drinking.

He busied himself sneaking forbidden peeks to see if the cold air from the refrigerator had further defined those dazzling nipples when he realized that Katie was speaking to him. He remembered so well the taste of those nipples, the feel of his lips around them, the tiny moans she hadn't stifled as he suckled them.

"Pardon?" He tried to mask his inattentiveness.

"I asked if you would care for a glass of wine."

He surrendered easily. "I shouldn't 'cause I've got practice early in the morning, but what the hell." He was fighting too many battles within himself to argue about a glass of wine.

Nevertheless, she looked alarmed.

"No problem," he assured her as he headed down the center passage to the tiny bathroom. "Let me wash up a little and we'll have some wine and some of that delicious-smelling meal, and everything will be fine."

Katie, bustling around in the tiny kitchen area, smiled

again and looked relieved, as if maybe she believed him.

Silly girl, he chided her in silence. *If you had a brain in that beautiful head of yours, you'd know that nothing is ever going to be fine again. I'm lying through my teeth.*

Chapter 8

Ian was *détraqué!*

Katriana searched her English vocabulary for a suitable equivalent. *Crazy,* perhaps. That was as close as she could come, although *crazy* seemed to carry the connotation of mental instability, and she hoped to *la Sante Vierge* that he wasn't mentally unstable. His particular *démence* leaned more toward failure to grasp her confusion at this new and bizarre life she found herself living. She might as well be trying to survive on the moon as tramping through the less civilized portions of the American South, wearing a billed cap and clothes off the rack.

Besides that, she was living in a bus! A lovely, comfortable, elegant sort of a bus, to be sure. But still a bus!

The strangeness of her new life seemed to close in around her, trapping her, strangling her, and she was bad-tempered. Perhaps it would have been better if she had obeyed her father and married Sir Christian.

Ugh! She shuddered.

No. No, indeed. Anything was better than that. Anything was better than Sir Christian's knarled hands skimming over her body, up and down her arms, across her shoulders, stroking her cheek, patting her hand.

But now Ian expected her to sleep in the same bed with him.

That was perhaps unkindest of all. He had shown not the

133

slightest interest in her since that rainy night in the front seat of his car at Cooter's. Was he so unaffected by her that he could slumber through the night with her stretched out beside him?

"*Non, non,*" she insisted, piqued by his lack of consideration for her sense of privacy and, even more than that, for his lack of interest in her in general. "Indeed not!"

In truth, lack of privacy was not a consideration. Her reactions to this man were fierce, impossible to suppress. And they led to nothing, which left her out of sorts, perplexed and hurt, aiming rude and hateful thoughts at a man who didn't deserve them.

Or did he?

"For crying out loud, Katie," he snapped, losing patience with her reticence. "The couch is barely four feet long! Neither one of us could fit on it without hanging over on both ends. I need my sleep, so crawl your butt up in the bed and do it now. Your virtue, such as it is, is safe with me tonight. I promise." His voice carried a new and nasty sneer that she didn't like at all.

Did this man not realize that her reticence had nothing to do with her *virtue*—and what did *such as it is* mean? Whatever it meant, it didn't sound at all nice.

"For God's sake, Katie, this bed is as big as a barn. I had it made just so I could . . ." He stopped and refused to finish sharing his reasons for wanting a vast monster of a bed. She almost feared to hear what he might have said. That imposing bed occupied almost the entire width of the bedroom in the back part of Ian's bus.

His black-and-red bedroom.

Katie had never encountered such a huge bed, nor such a vibrant combination of colors as Ian had chosen for that bedroom.

Perhaps Ian's nasty temper sprang from his exhaustion; he'd been almost gray with pain and fatigue when he had returned to the bus earlier for dinner that evening. And hungry, too, based on how he ate. How fortunate that she had found fully cooked food for sale at a nearby market. Then she had experimented and determined exactly what particular functions the various knobs and switches on the microwave oven were meant to control. In the end, she had presented him with a rather edible dinner.

Ian wolfed it all down with the same gusto she herself had shown for the potato-and-frozen-burrito dinner he had prepared for her.

Afterwards he relaxed a little, sipped his wine, and made polite conversation and his manners were impeccable, yet he refused to meet her gaze. Katriana found his behavior incredibly annoying. A few nights ago, she had done her duty to him, and she found his embarrassment to be . . . well, she found it to be embarrassing.

In the end, the evening had culminated when he insisted that she crawl into bed with him, and specifically mentioned her butt!

But over an hour later, she was still flouncing around in the huge bed, seeking a comfortable position, turning to face first one way, then the other, restless, unable to fall sleep. She could try blaming her current distress on insomnia, but the fact remained that Ian lay mere inches from her—wearing nothing but his underwear.

She felt the bed flex under his weight as he moved around in his own restless pursuit of a comfortable position.

He was so close. If he reached out to touch her, wrap his arms around her, draw her close to his own body . . .

She swallowed and fought to control her ragged attempts to breathe. Her reactions to this man were uncontrollable—

humiliating, actually. She felt things for him, wanted things from him, things that she had never before imagined. Wild and wanton things. Things buried deep inside of her that demanded to be explored and set free.

As the slow minutes passed, she grew aware of certain parts of her body she had ignored until that night. Her breasts felt strange and heavy, as if they might be blossoming, reaching out to Ian, hoping he would touch them, stroke them.

Her nipples grew unbearably sensitive as they punched like tight little pellets against the silk of her new sleeping gown, purchased on her shopping expedition that day. Even the slight weight of the silk brushing across their beaded tips tingled like a caress.

Low in her stomach, a potent and unfamiliar tension curled, shooting out ferocious bolts of energy to that most unmentionable part of her body, that lower, feminine place.

If Ian sought her as a proper husband would, she knew that she would go to him eagerly. Her body clenched with anticipation at the very thought.

Her heart was racing.

Her body was pulsing.

And her husband was snoring!

Twelve hours later, sweltering in the South Carolina heat, standing atop the huge truck that carried his racecars from track to track, Ian added a new trick to his repertoire of idiosyncrasies that drove her crazy.

"Okay, Katie, showtime," he whispered. His breath tickled her ear, and other places that were nowhere near her ear. She needed to come to terms with her attraction to this strange man who seemed to care nothing about her. Yet he could play the part of the besotted husband very well when it suited his purposes. Mere seconds ago, when he'd first spied the group of reporters flocking toward them, he had gently swept her around in front of him and wrapped her in his arms.

Very confusing. But at the same time, quite wonderful!

Before Ian had decided it was time he acted amorously, they were watching some sort of a race at the track where he was scheduled to race the following day. He kept fiddling with a double stopwatch, timing various cars as they circled the track. Some of the results brought out his devastating smile, while others caused him to frown and mutter.

Katriana fanned herself with a piece of paper and vowed to check a map of the United States at her first opportunity. She had no memory of parts of this country being located anywhere near the Equator. In fact, she had no idea what latitude she was in. All she knew was that wherever she was, she was far from the fresh, dry breezes of the Mediterranean.

Darlington, South Carolina looked nothing like a rain forest, yet it surely felt like one. She silently thanked Ian for having the forethought to buy her a few pairs of shorts at that awful K-Market place in Atlanta. She would have wilted and died today in jeans. She was also thankful for the large-brimmed straw hat she'd bought herself the day before, along with a few necessities like presentable lingerie and sleeping attire. After all, a lady was known by her lingerie, or so Monique had instructed her.

"You just smile and look pretty. Keep your hat pulled down as far as you can, and don't say a damned word," Ian ordered. He gave a last-minute tug on her new straw hat, no doubt ruining the elegant angle at which she had it tilted. Then he waved to the gaggle of reporters congregating just below them.

"Oh, yeah. We're supposed to be blissfully just-married, so . . ." He tilted her chin up, turned her face toward him, and dropped a quick kiss on her lips. His lips moved against hers, the tip of his tongue brushed across her lips, and then he drew away, searching her face—for something. Consent, perhaps? Alarm? She had no idea what he was looking for, or if he found it. But then he shook his head.

She clung to the brief hope that she was on the verge of receiving another kiss—with any luck a better, more forceful kiss than the previous one—but it was not to be.

"Hey, Ian," one of the reporters called up to him. The man sounded cordial, but Katriana didn't trust him, or any other reporter. All her life, she had been schooled to distrust the paparazzi.

"Long time no see," Ian called back. He smiled and his words sounded cordial enough, but she sensed the hint of steel underlying his tone. "What are you guys up to? Surely, I'm not bigger news now that I've got a pretty, new wife than I was lying half-dead in the hospital, am I?"

After some embarrassed foot-shuffling by the annoying reporters, followed by a spurt of nervous laughter, the spokesman called up, "Hell, Ian, you weren't in any shape to be interviewed back in February." The man stopped to smile at his own attempt at a joke before he continued. Katriana found it in poor taste. "We had to pack up and head for the next race in Rockingham. You know how it is. No hanging around or you get left behind."

"Oh, I know all about getting left behind, believe me," Ian came back. He even chuckled, but his voice kept its steel undertone. There was no question about who was in charge of this particular interview.

"Your wreck got a hell of a write-up. You know that," the reporter continued. "Pictures of the fire. Pictures of you half-dead on a stretcher. Pictures of the helicopter flying off with you in it. It was huge stuff, buddy. Big spread all over the papers the next day. Really good stuff. Didn't you see it?"

"Some of it," Ian confirmed. "But I sure as hell didn't see it the next day. I was a little busy the next day, unconscious, and for a bunch of next days after that."

The reporters shuffled uncomfortably.

"So, boys, I guess you came to meet my wife. Well, here she is." Ian broke the uncomfortable silence himself. Katriana watched a sea of pads and pens snap to attention below her.

Immediately the questions began. "How long you two been married?"

"A while," Ian answered.

That was obviously not the answer they were seeking.

"How long have you two known each other?"

"A little longer than we've been married."

There was a hint of muttering below.

"Where did you two meet?"

"Now, fellows, that's a little personal, isn't it?"

Katriana smiled. Ian was answering questions while saying nothing.

"Reckon you could give us a quote, Miz—say, what's your name anyway, honey?"

"Her name is Mrs. Grayson, and if I were you, that's what I'd call her," Ian advised them. "By the way, just a quick word of advice—any of you with any brains in your head won't be calling her *honey.*"

"What about a quote, Mrs. Grayson?" the reporter asked, undaunted, yet attempting to follow Ian's rules, such as they were.

"She doesn't have much to say right now, I don't think, do you, sweetheart?" Ian announced, but he pretended to look to her for confirmation.

He still stood behind her, hugging her to him, trying out a

139

new trick that he had surely designed to drive her insane right there in front of the annoying paparazzi. As the reporters continued to pelt him with questions, he tossed his answers back to them, all the time keeping her wrapped in his arms and continuing to drop tiny yet earth-shattering kisses on the back of her neck . . . the side of her neck . . . under her ear... That was quite a sensitive place, she discovered.

He surely felt her racing heart too, what with his hand lying so close to it. He chuckled into her ear, dropped another of those tiny, blazing kisses on her neck, bantering back and forth with the reporters and yielding no information concerning his new wife.

Ian Grayson was indeed a man of many talents.

Chapter 9

Perhaps, in the end, it was the fault of the hamburger. But hamburgers didn't render one crazy and prone to regrettable decisions.

"Want to get some burgers?" Ian asked as soon as they had returned to the bus from his interview. The clever way he'd handled the press must have been more difficult than it looked. Ian was hungry.

"I don't know. I've never eaten a hamburger." Katriana was aware of her shortcomings in this strange, new world of American culture. She was, of course, familiar with hamburgers in general, but such things had never been served at the palace.

Ian muttered something that sounded blasphemous, which she disregarded.

"Well, do you want to give it a try, or should I go out and look for some pickled octopus under glass or whatever the hell you people eat?"

"A hamburger will be more than sufficient," she replied.

Ian looked as if he might be about to apologize for his rudeness, but in the end he didn't. He stared at her in silence for a long moment, then instructed her to stay inside with the door locked, out of sight of the reporters, while he went in search of hamburgers.

When he returned thirty minutes later with a sackful of burgers, they smelled divine but . . .

"This looks quite dreadful."

Those were her first, and quite unappreciated, words as she prodded the soggy bun with its mushy lump of *boeuf* topped with a pile of salad.

Ian glared at her and then went about demonstrating, complete with *ooh-ing* and *ahh-ing,* how delicious he found hamburgers.

Katriana followed his lead and cautiously nibbled one. It tasted a bit better than it looked, but she wasn't very hungry and the bread seemed to stick in her throat. She still had trouble forcing herself to touch her food with her hands, but that seemed *de rigeur* when eating a hamburger, so she tried very hard to comply.

Despite Ian's great show of how much he loved hamburgers, Katriana noticed that he ate almost nothing. He was much more interested in guzzling the beer he'd brought back.

In the short time she had spent with him, Katriana had developed a surprising penchant for chilled beer. Beer with her hamburger was delicious, but it presented a new problem.

"Surely you're not supposed drink beer the night before you race, are you?" She inquired, but even to her own ears it sounded more like a lecture than a question.

"A couple won't hurt." Ian had the look of an embarrassed child caught in a lie.

She realized that she should have stood her ground, but Ian looked so distressed that she hushed and watched him drink one beer followed by another.

As the evening wore on, he grew fidgety and distracted.

He couldn't sit still.

He wandered back and forth, in and out of the bedroom.

He tried to watch television, but promptly switched it off when the local announcer started previewing the next day's race.

He flopped around on the couch and pretended to read the newspaper.

But soon he was up and pacing again, this time with that jerky gait that announced that his back, or his leg, or both, were troubling him.

Clearly he was tired and sore from crawling in and out of the car—practicing, readying himself and the car for tomorrow's race. She could see it in his eyes. But there was something else lurking in those chocolate eyes. She'd seen the pain before, and the fatigue. They had spent enough time together that she now knew Ian Grayson well enough to read his moods.

The new mood she read was one that she had encountered before in this man, briefly, as they sat watching the video of his horrible wreck at Daytona.

That mood was fear.

Fear.

Ian had no experience dealing with fear. Even now, all he knew of it was how much he hated the sweaty, sick feeling, the thumping heart and sensation of a bottomless, never-ending freefall that came with it.

His fear lay like a massive lump stretching from his throat to his stomach, with the few bites of hamburger he had choked down lying on top of it.

He had tasted fear in small, preliminary doses each time he watched the tape of his wreck, but those tiny tidbits barely scratched the surface of the hell he currently inhabited.

Tomorrow he would climb back into the car and race, actually *race.*

Not just practice, which was nothing. *Nothing!* His practice times were dismal for no other reason than he couldn't force himself to accelerate. When it came time to qualify, he and his car were all alone on the track and he had blistered off one of his better qualifying efforts in recent memory. But when the rest of the cars were dumped back into the equation, the result was something much less than a competitive speed.

He twisted the cap off beer number three. Katie, in her khaki shorts and cherry-red top, with her tanned legs and elegant little feet folded under her as she sat on one end of the couch, shot him yet another of the disapproving glances she'd been perfecting all evening.

If she had any inkling of what was running through his head, her disapproval would shoot straight up to the level of condemnation. As if drowning in fear weren't bad enough, he had made the grave mistake of trying to dilute his panic with a good old-fashioned dose of fantasy.

Terror was a painful thing indeed, but so was his unrelieved hunger for Katie.

He couldn't bear to think about tomorrow because it might very well be the day that he died. He couldn't bear to think about his unsuitable royal pain of a wife because he was terrified of falling in love with her. For sure, they had no chance in hell of any kind of a future as a couple.

He turned away from the sight of Katie on the couch watching him reproachfully and trudged back down the short hallway on yet another trip to the bedroom. He squelched those fantasies about making love to her. They were counter-productive. Except that they *did* divert his mind from tomorrow's race . . . the race that might kill him, or cripple him, or turn him into a vegetable, or . . .

Aw, hell, there he went off on THAT part of the damned merry-go-round again. Crazy, stupid painted horses, circling all around him like Indians dancing around a wagon train . . . dipping down into the shadowy gloom of his own thoughts . . .

144

A nervous shiver rippled through him and he cursed his own weakness.

There was nothing in the bedroom to hold his interest, just like the last eight times he had wandered in there. He swigged yet another long, cool gulp of beer and turned around to wander back toward the living room . . . to Katie . . .

. . . *and those hellacious merry-go-round horses on the upswing, trying to soar like his heart every single time she said his name.*

"Ian, you must sit down," she informed him. "*Ici.* Right here beside me." She patted the couch seat next to her. "And you must stop drinking beer."

Her speech, her inflection, her gestures, every blessed ounce of her, was so unlike anything he had ever known. So intriguing. So fetching and charming. So damned arousing he wondered how he was going to live through the rest of the evening.

The rest of the night.

He had no business anywhere near her in the shape he was in. If he somehow managed not to snap in two from the pre-race tension, he would surely pounce on her and make a fool of himself—again.

Why was it so hard for him to remember that this woman was the big time? He had no doubt that she'd banged her way through the heirs-apparent of every surviving royal house of Europe, with a movie star or two thrown in when life got dull.

So why was he now sitting, docile and accommodating, right beside her, exactly as she had instructed him?

Like a lamb headed straight to its slaughter. Like a moth unable to resist the flame.

Destiny calling.

And there he sat, poor Ian Grayson, facing his own mortality, caught in an avalanche of desire for her, fresh out of willpower.

★ ★ ★ ★ ★

"Your poor back is one big knot," she admonished, kneading diligently at a lump of knotted muscles. Rubbing Ian's back was the least she could do for him. He was obviously in pain.

He grunted as she pushed and worked at the little worms of tension surrounding his left shoulder blade.

But whatever she did, with whatever skill and precision she massaged his back, he refused to relax, until . . .

"Oh, God, Katie, that feels like heaven," he groaned as she turned her attention to the muscles up each side of his neck.

How quickly she had grown accustomed to being *Katie,* to finding comfort in the presence of this stranger who was also her husband—*kind* of her husband—and the new, American name he had given her. Each day her feelings for him intensified. Exactly what those feelings were, she couldn't say, because she'd never known such feelings before.

Ian was kind and generous. *And he was sexy!* Her experience with *sexy* was lacking, but what she knew of it, she liked.

Another experience she liked was rubbing his back, the substantial feel of him, the warmth and vitality that seeped from him, the inexplicable sensations that ripped through her from touching him.

Up both sides of his neck, then back down, across his shoulders, she worked with diligence and patience.

Ian shrugged those impressive shoulders forward as she made her way from the tip of one all the way across his back to the tip of the other. She was certain that he liked it because he lolled his head back and groaned again.

"You must take better care of yourself," she scolded.

"Yes, ma'am."

She rose up on her knees behind him for better leverage,

pressing the pads of her thumbs carefully into either side of the back of his neck. She worked in silence, except for the random grunts he emitted each time she homed in on a sensitive spot.

"Quite the little masseuse, aren't we?" he noted as she worked her fingers up into and through the hair at the base of his skull.

His entire body rippled with a shiver.

She did it again and he responded with another shiver. This time she realized that those shivers were involuntary responses, because he cleared his throat and squirmed around as if embarrassed.

"I have studied *le massage.*"

"I'll just bet you have, Princess," he answered, his head bowed to allow better access to that very tense place where his neck joined his shoulders. His words seemed ill-mannered, but his low, rich chuckle softened their impact.

He was flirting with her! She could hear it in his voice. A blush crept up her neck, then to her face, and she was glad that Ian faced the opposite direction and couldn't see her discomfort. She made a great effort to ignore the blush and its implications as she continued her work on his knotted muscles.

But the mood was now different. A new awareness settled over her. Despite her best intentions, he now felt strange and foreign beneath her touch. Her hands longed to skim his body, not therapeutically, but to learn its shape and feel. She allowed them to graze down the long muscles of his back, then all the way back up to his neck, and finally to slide again through his hair.

Where moments ago he'd shivered as she massaged his head, he now flinched from her touch as if trying to avoid an open flame.

Her hands skimmed down his neck to his shoulders, across their breadth, then up again.

Another flinch and he muttered "Jesus" under his breath. All the tension she had massaged from his body returned *en masse,* rippling up and down his back. Then, with no warning at all, he turned and kissed her.

Oh, yes, indeed, Ian Grayson was a skillful kisser. Never had she doubted that. Their first kiss—*her* first kiss ever—had been alarming but in its own way wonderful.

Their second real kiss, the one in the darkened car on their rainy wedding night in Atlanta—because that dry, powdery nothing of a kiss at their wedding earlier that day didn't really count as a kiss—was a revelation of all that she'd missed. She had tried very hard to reciprocate, to show him, with the skills Monique had instilled in her, that she cared for him. But, ultimately, her affection had only angered him.

Then yesterday he had dropped that tiny, third after-thought of a kiss on her lips as they played happy newlyweds for the paparazzi. That particular kiss had been confusing. It lay in some no-man's-wasteland between *not nearly enough* and *much too much* to endure before the gaggle of nosy strangers.

And now their fourth kiss. His lips captured and held hers with rare and unexpected magic. This was the kiss she would remember forever. Not the unexpected first one. Nor the crazy second one. Or even the confusing third one. It was *this* one, the one where they met as equals.

He plundered her eager mouth and half-turned himself toward her as she knelt behind him on the couch. His hands crept up and cradled her face, her chin . . . then lower . . .

Before the kiss had flamed out, she was seated in his lap.

"I've tried like you'll never believe, but I can't fight it any more," he whispered as he drew her into his arms, turned her around in his lap so she was facing him, atop his . . .

Mon dieu! One straddled a horse. One did *not* straddle another person. Such a position was quite improper—yet thrilling.

The hard bulge of his desire rested at the apex of her splayed legs, separated from the center of her own throbbing desire by a few scant layers of clothing. She had no doubt that Ian had planned it so, most especially when he urged her, encouraged her to move herself against him.

Excitement, desperate and demanding, flooded through her. She craved the ultimate intimacy, with no barriers between them.

She moved once more against him. He rose under her to sustain the connection.

"Your leg," she mumbled around the heat of his kiss. "We mustn't hurt your leg."

"To hell with my leg," he muttered. "I've got bigger problems right now than a gimpy leg." Again, he rubbed the physical proof of those *bigger problems* against her.

He allowed his hands free rein to find their way under her shirt and roam across her stomach, trailing rippling shocks of liquid desire in their wake. He loosened her bra, then covered her breasts, and spent some memorable minutes exploring and re-acquainting himself with them. Then back down her body, with one of his impertinent hands dipping below and under the loose waistband of her shorts . . . lower . . . heart-stoppingly lower . . . until he brushed the center of her universe. Ashamed, yet unable to control herself, she ground herself against him. He cradled her intimately, stroked, then he moved on and dipped his brazen and knowledgeable finger inside of her.

She gasped at the sheer delight of it. Ian stopped kissing her and watched her intently, his eyes no longer chocolate-brown, but impenetrable and bottomless. His own body moved itself under and against her with the rhythm of his fingers as they explored

Once . . .

Again . . .

Mon dieu, something immense began . . . built . . . roared . . .

Her body clenched, her head dropped back, her length of hair brushing across her shoulders and down her back.

Again.

His touch was no more than a flutter against her yet it encompassed her entire world.

She knew she groaned because she heard herself. Embarrassment flooded her, yet she could do nothing to stop the immense, life-altering wave from engulfing her. She bore down hard against him, moved with him, groaned once again . . .

. . . and fell off the edge of the world.

Ian's arms were deliciously full of Katie. Her face lay buried in the crook of his neck, her body still vibrating with the tiny aftershocks of her climax—right there in his lap! And, heaven help him, he was tottering on the verge himself.

He wanted to draw this moment out, savor it. His deepest wish was to make their connection go beyond *mating*. He had *mated* before, and often, and whatever pleasure he found from the act was, at best, momentary and superficial. With Katie, there should be more—of everything.

But did he have enough finesse—or even patience—to pour into this experience everything it should contain? Already he shook with urgency, dragging him close to his point of no return.

Katie's breathing slowed and she leaned back to stare at

him, her eyes questioning.

She was a complex little thing. The only point of reference they shared was that they both breathed air and needed water and nourishment to survive.

He loved her!

He could never tell her, but he did. He didn't like anything about it, but he could do nothing to stop it. From the minute he'd perceived the attraction, he'd done his damnedest to distance himself emotionally from her at the same time he had taken care to keep her physically at his side so he could protect her.

What could he offer this fairy tale princess? She was perfection and he was flawed—physically, emotionally, his career, every damned thing about him. Yet here she sat, trembling on his lap, her eyes boring into his, asking strange, silent, cryptic questions that he couldn't understand.

Need thundered through him with such savagery that he ached with the force of it.

"I want you, Katie," he whispered. "I want you so bad I don't think I can stand it."

"I am aware," she murmured, sounding so French, so foreign, so enchanting. Yet at the same time so very proper and unsuitable for him and the only kind of life he could offer her.

Of course, she was aware. How could she not be?

He leaned forward across the few inches that separated them and kissed her again. That kiss was heaven. Her hands, cool and soft, crept up and cradled his face, slid along his scalp and zinged him from the top of his head to the tips of his toes. He gathered her in his arms and prayed she wouldn't do much more scooting around in his lap until they finished that kiss. He wanted to lose himself in the luxury of it, not focus all his energy on holding on to the shreds of his control.

Had he ever really kissed a woman like this before? He sure

as hell thought he had, but it had never been this intimate. Time ground to a halt. Katie wrapped her arms around him and kissed him crazy. She was incredibly responsive, yet her kisses had a dainty, almost elegant aspect to them that appealed to him. No big, wet, slurpy kisses for Her Highness, the Princess of Île d'Arinedra.

He eased her down so she lay stretched out on the sofa. He needed to see her, to feast his eyes on the sight of this beautiful, unattainable woman who, despite his best intentions, was bound, within the next few minutes, to become his wife in every possible way. Life was too short to deny himself the pleasures of her body. *Particularly his life!* It might all end tomorrow, but he refused to fall into his grave without first making love to Katie.

In his mind he freed himself to tell her of his love, all those words he could never allow himself to say. To let her know what a difference she had made not only in his life but also in the way he viewed himself. To thank her for reviving emotions that he had given up as dead along with his marriage. Rusty, almost-forgotten feelings of self-worth. Feelings that transcended sex.

But sex demanded its own rank in the whirlwind consuming him. He had desired this woman from the moment he saw her and he would have her now, tonight, and for however long she decided to stay with him until her problems were resolved and she chose to go back to her other—her real—life. Maybe before she left, if he lived through tomorrow and his crushing fear of what might happen then, he could separate their complicated relationship into its natural and logical components.

In the meantime, Katie was so many confusing things. She was funny and sweet. She was hurt and afraid. She was shy. She was enchanting. She was resilient. For a girl who had been raised by nuns, she had a genuine flair for cussing when the mood struck her. She needed him as no one had ever needed him before. And she ought to be outraged that a nobody like him would dare to hope that she would act as a receptacle for his passion. But she wasn't.

He hated his overriding physical needs and the way they ruled his life. Yet at the same time he damned them, he could almost hear himself whining and begging them to hurry him along on his blissful way toward that ultimate moment of sexual connection with Katie.

As he leaned over her to indulge himself in yet another of her kisses, he felt her hands seek his zipper. In seconds she had worked him free of the painful confines of his jeans, murmuring to him in French. He had no idea what she said . . . or even if it was complimentary. What he *did* know was that it was incredibly arousing to a man who rode the narrow line between sanity and insanity.

She stoked him again as she had the night in the car in Cooter's parking lot, but he couldn't allow that. He could hardly spare the time or energy to finish shedding his pants.

Not as gently as he might have hoped, he peeled Katie's shorts and elegant, lacy underthings from her and tossed them aside. His desperate need to be inside of her, to pour himself into her—to connect and meld and become a part of her—overrode every good and decent instinct still in him.

He clenched his teeth and vowed that the next time he would be gentler. He wouldn't be so over-the-edge wild. He would take whatever time he needed to savor her, and carefully bring her along with him as he called upon his inventory of lovemaking skills. The next time he wouldn't be staring down death's ugly throat.

If there was a next time . . .

The gateway to her body beckoned as he knelt between her

parted legs. Physical urgency and his desperate fears drove him on without mercy.

He entered her . . . roughly . . . nothing gentle about it.

She was unbelievably tight!

And, dammit to hell, in his overwhelming rush, his angle of entrance—something—was wrong.

His burning, aching need for release made him crazy . . . wild. He could barely restrain himself and he wasn't even inside her yet.

This was not the way a man made love to the woman he loved. But he was out of control, riding a wave, almost finished before he could even get started.

He drew back and plunged into her again. Harder . . . straighter . . . but not much deeper. Then, thankfully, the obscure resistance gave away and he drove himself home.

He had no thought or time to waste on anything but his ferocious, roaring urgency. He stroked long and hard once, then again. Katie groaned a short, guttural grunt, but then relaxed, sighed, and started to move in rhythm with him, which spurred him on to wilder heights.

Faster . . . deeper . . . stronger . . . again and again.

He plunged, buried himself, and groaned out loud as hot jets of scalding passion burst from him.

He wanted to wallow in the joy of the moment forever. But, of course, it couldn't last, so he tried to tuck it away inside himself to be reclaimed and revisited, assuming he managed somehow to live past tomorrow.

But even that searing rush of perfection wasn't enough to heat the chill gripping his vital parts.

There was very little in his life of which he could be proud. But on this night, even as he had longed to create enough memories to warm the lonely nights he saw dotting whatever future he might have, he'd stooped to a new low. And the horror of what he'd done was almost paralyzing in its intensity.

In his lust and his selfish, arrogant, raging need, he'd damned the consequences—once again misreading the clues —and taken Katie's virginity.

What—if anything—had he been thinking?

For some inexplicable reason, Katie lay snuggled, soft and drowsy against him. Christ, she should be kicking and screaming, clawing holes his face. If he had any redeeming qualities, he ought to kick and scream and claw his own face on her behalf, since he doubted she'd been bred to brawl with commoners.

When had he become such a flaming asshole? How could he have committed such an atrocity?

And why had Katie allowed him to do it?

Instead of slapping the shit out of him as she should have done, she'd been willing, almost eager. A virgin, trusting and placing her faith in him—no-good SOB that he was—to treat her with consideration and respect.

So what had he done in return? He'd screwed her. Flipped her over on her back and pounded himself into her with enough lack of restraint to shame a bull elk in full rut.

He'd thundered forward, ignoring the obvious physical barrier to his first impatient thrusts. Hell, even a pimply-faced sixteen-year-old should have recognized that resistance for what it was. So why didn't the almighty Ian Grayson, the man who had made love to more women than he could even keep track of?

Because he had no experience with virgins, that's why. Not even Cheryl, his teenaged bride. Not even his first experience. Not even anybody, anywhere, ever. Until Katie.

Leave. Run like hell and don't look back.

He ignored the voice in his head, and clutched her tighter, buried his face in her hair, twined his leg around hers like a sprout of ivy. When had he ever listened to that voice anyway? Especially when it warned him about Katie.

He would do well to pay attention to it because it worked overtime, trying its damnedest to keep him out of trouble. *Don't get involved,* it had insisted back in Daytona Beach when he heard the commotion next door. But he ignored it. Too busy jumping into his pants, in record time considering his bum leg, so he could hobble right on over like the fool that he was, to check things out, to be helpful and polite. Ignoring every grain of his better judgment.

Sealing Katie's fate.

He wondered if God might show him some mercy if he raised the defense of tabloid-gossip-overload. After all, those supermarket rags were filled with torrid tales of Princess Katriana's white-hot sexual liaisons. He could remember, without even looking, the names of at least seven of her world-famous mythical partners. Of course, he now knew she hadn't done any such thing with those men or anyone else. But he'd believed every word written about her. Their entire time together he'd hurled nasty sexual innuendoes at her, made tacky jokes about her supposed conquests then grew cranky when she had no idea what he was talking about.

Oh, yeah, he was such a clever guy.

Did Île d'Arinedra have an army? And if so, was it possible that army had been sworn to inflict a bloody and hideous death on any man who dared do what Ian had just done to its virgin princess?

He should have shown infinite care and sensitivity for her. After all, even as he took unfair advantage of her body, he admitted to himself that he loved her. Yet he continued to shove forward with crude and selfish haste.

So, yes, if the Île d'Arinedra storm troopers showed up with a platter for transporting his head back to Katie's already-pissed-off father, he had no defense at all to offer.

What were the chances, he wondered, of encouraging those potential executioners to arrange their schedules so they could show up sometime before the race commenced tomorrow morning? At least he would be spared the humiliation of wrecking again horribly and dying on television as the world watched.

Katie shifted beneath him and he repositioned himself to protect his groin, his most vulnerable part. If Her Highness was as furious with him as she ought to be, she could have him singing soprano with one lucky knee shot.

Even if she kicked his nuts all the way across the room and back, it was still less than he deserved.

For the moment, however, all parts below the belt seemed safe enough because Katie only flexed her back then nestled against him again. Her body felt warm and familiar. Her fingers played up and down along his back with lazy and casual ease. Lord, did she even realize she was caressing him?

He loved her touch. He craved it. He soaked it up and silently begged for more before his body took control again. Soon he would be forced to move away before he went stupid and made love to her again. This was a one-time shot and that was what it must remain.

Katie deserved better than him. He had nothing at all to offer her except a bit of temporary shelter from her father, and even that was suspect if he faced the truth. He was no superhero or much of anything else, except a poor excuse for a racecar driver who was afraid to drive.

As Tarzan would have advised Jane if they had met under these unlikely circumstances:

"You Princess."

"Me nobody."

He would be wise to keep that in mind no matter how

desirable she was.

No matter how much he loved her.

There had been a bit of pain, but nothing so *odieux* as it might have been.

Monique had skimmed over that part quickly because— and she had been quite frank about it—she did not suspect that Sir Christian would be capable of consummation.

Monique had not prepared her for Ian Grayson.

Moments before, she had experienced something profound and thrilling, something almost indescribable in its intensity. That must be the very essence of life, the secret something that happened between men and women that inspired poems and wars, toppled kingdoms, spurred people to risk their lives, and their hearts, for each other. It was the physical embodiment of love.

Ian's voice broke through her reveries, husky and choked, with no preamble.

"Why didn't you tell me?"

Katie was unsure what words she had expected from Ian, but those were not the words. Nor did he kiss her again as she wished he would. The fact that she was naked began to intrude on her sense of joy at what had occurred between them. She tried to recapture some small scrap of her dignity but it was very difficult lying naked, beneath him on the tiny couch in his bus, with *stuff* dripping from her.

Minutes ago, Ian had been so *romantique.* So bold and skilled. But now he was different, almost removed.

"Why didn't I tell you what?"

"Katie, surely even you realized where this was headed. Didn't you think it might be important to mention that you were still a virgin?"

"A virgin?" she repeated, unsure where the conversation

was headed. "Why would that surprise you?

He frowned but didn't respond.

"You know that I have never before been married," she continued.

"I'm not sure what that has to do with anything." He frowned.

"I would suspect that it has to do with virtue and the sanctity of marriage," she replied.

Ian stood up, located his jeans then pulled them on and zipped them in short, determined, jerky movements. His face was set and rigid. She had the unsettling sense that he was holding back tears. She longed to approach him and try to comfort away whatever was disturbing him, but she was unsure of her welcome. Even though she had now been intimate with this man, there were so many aspects of him she could not relate to or understand.

"I was confused about some important things, Katie," he said. "You'll have to cut me a little slack on all this. But let's be up front with each other and not get caught up in technicalities. OK? I'll even start the ball rolling by agreeing that until today you've somehow kept from doing the big nasty. But then I expect you to return the favor and agree that you're not quite as innocent as you seem."

Why did he look as if he were begging her to concede this peculiar point? What possible meaning could it have for him? Was he trying in some way to salve his conscience?

"And what, pray tell, is *the big nasty?*" she asked, bewildered, hurt, yet her head held at full, regal tilt, as she had been taught to do. "Perhaps it is best to ignore that question. I am not sure that I care to know," she finished with a haughty sniff and a toss of her hair. She doubted that she had conveyed quite the sense of dignity she was seeking. Pawing around on the floor half-naked, in search of her discarded clothes left a bit to be desired in the way of decorum.

One does not stoop to justify oneself to the masses, Katriana, her governess had instructed her many times. *One merely freezes the challenger and moves on.*

"I can't stay here with you," he stated, his voice flat and lifeless. He turned away and busied himself with locating the shirt he had discarded earlier with such haste.

"Why?"

"We should have never made love, especially with you not—never—till now—" He stopped speaking and raked his hand through his hair. "If I'd known you were—you know—I would never have touched you."

"I had no idea virginity was such a loathsome state," she countered, embarrassed for reasons she couldn't understand. Why should she feel embarrassment for retaining her virginity until she surrendered it to her husband? Although she dared not look at him, she felt the full force of his eyes boring into her back.

Yes, indeed they were, she learned when she found the nerve to turn and face him.

"Please don't insult me by pretending complete innocence, Katie. I'll vouch that technically this was your first time. But I'd also have to add a disclaimer that you've got some of the most excellent hand-jive moves of any woman I've ever known."

The term *hand jive* meant nothing to her, until he clarified with a crude gesture.

"In the car at Cooter's. And please don't look confused like I just lapsed into Swahili. You know exactly what I'm talking about."

"Monique taught me many . . ."

"Excuse me," he interrupted. "Did I hear you right?" He stared at her in disbelief. "Monique? A woman? Surely to heaven, you're not involved with a woman, are you?"

Katriana felt color rush up her neck and flood her face.

"Of course, I am not *involved* with a woman," she tried to clarify. "Monique is a courtesan employed by my father who instructed me in the proper—"

"A courtesan? Are you telling me that your father hired a hooker to teach you about sex?"

"Not exactly about sex, as such," she continued to attempt to explain. "More specifically how to pleasure a man of Sir Christian's years."

"That's sick."

"I don't recall you finding it so sick the other night in the car," she answered, then hurried on, blushing at his incredulous look and her own implication. "Monique's techniques were quite therapeutic for you too, were they not?"

"Therapeutic?"

"For your impotence. You were cured right there in that car. In your very first session. And now, tonight, you have demonstrated that you can again function normally."

"Function normally?" Ian looked as if he might collapse. "What the hell is *function normally* supposed to mean?"

"It means, of course, what you just did," she tried to explain what was, for her, unexplainable.

"What on earth did you think was wrong with me?" he asked, disbelief and confusion evident in his eyes, his stiff carriage, the way he shook his head *no* over and over again. "I don't have any problems like that. I can *function normally* in my sleep."

"That is another problem entirely, Ian," she informed him, not daring to look at him at she drew from her store of knowledge imparted by Monique. "It occurs most often in adolescent boys, I believe."

"I don't have any sexual dysfunctions," he snapped. "I

can't believe that you thought I did."

She said nothing.

He scraped both hands down his face. Was he frustrated, uncomfortable? Well, he *should* be. She certainly was. "So don't think you've done me any favors in that area."

"Heaven forbid," she murmured.

"Please stop that," he said.

"Stop what?"

"Stop being haughty and snobby."

Her only response to such nonsense was an insolent sniff.

"You did trick me. You have to admit that you did."

"No, Ian. *En vérité,* I did not trick you."

"You had your hands all over me. You—" He stopped and looked pained. "I can't stop myself when you touch me. I can't control myself." His wonderful eyes met hers and held them. "I can't even be responsible for myself, Katie. How in the hell am I supposed to take care of you, too?"

She shook her head, because she had no answer.

"This wasn't supposed to be anything special. It was just supposed to be for a little while. No strings. No commitment. Nobody owing anything to anybody."

"Perhaps it can still be that way."

"Are you crazy?" he asked. He punctuated the question with what was supposed to be a laugh, but it sounded more like a croak. Or a broken sob. "Are you out of your mind?"

She shrugged.

"After—after *that?* Katie, that was immense—huge. That was off the scale. That was magic. And you know what? I can't handle it right now. I've done you a grave disservice by bringing you here. Giving you false hope that I'm some kind of white knight. I can't do it, Katie. I have to focus on whatever pieces of my career I can find and piece back together. I'm committed to race tomorrow and I'm not sure I can even force myself to climb into the car. I'm afraid, Katie. How's that for a knight in shining armor? I'm a dud. I don't have anything left over to give *you* because it's taking every ounce of energy I can find right now to simply face tomorrow. The bad guys out there are looking for you right now and I don't have a clue what to do if they show up. How in the hell can I protect you when I don't even have the courage to do the one thing in this world that I know how to do well enough to make a living—drive a racecar?"

"What do you mean?"

"I mean that I'm bailing out. Old Ian's gonna do what he does best. I'm gonna get on my pony and ride."

"But what about our marriage?"

"Your church doesn't even recognize it, Katie. Why should you? If you want to divorce me or annul it, or whatever you want to do, go ahead and do it. Please. Be my guest. I don't even have enough energy to fight you."

"But . . . but . . . I don't . . . I can't . . ." She felt herself start to fall apart, to disintegrate in the throes of fear and uncertainty so she stopped, took a deep breath and reached down inside herself to dredge up the secret, impenetrable part of herself that had never yet let her down.

"So where should I go?" she asked, and she sounded surprisingly rational despite the ragged fear clutching her insides. She had no money. She had no transportation. She had no idea where Darlington, South Carolina even was in the vast United States of America. So many problems to face and overcome, at the same time she was dealing with a broken heart.

Ian wasn't the only one facing an unbearable tomorrow.

Oh, mon dieu. She had driven him into this bottomless pit with her problems and her needs. She wanted to melt into the floor and sob for this flawed hero who had tried so hard to give of himself but found he had nothing left to give. But of course one must never cry, especially in the presence of others.

"I don't know the answer to that either, Katie. I just know that I can't live with you like this any more. Go back home. Tell them that you're damaged goods. I doubt that the old lech will want you after you've been with me. Maybe I did somehow bumble around and manage to do one good thing for you." He sounded so weary, nothing at all like the Ian Grayson she had come to know . . . and love.

"If you let me stay, I will make no demands at all. You will not be responsible for me. I will do nothing more than travel with you, secretly, out of sight." She didn't like the pleading tone she heard in her own voice.

"Damn it, Katie. Can't you see what you do to me? Don't you know that I can't be alone with you without needing to make love to you? Didn't what happened tonight give you any kind of clue as to what a complete and utter jerk I am? All you did was rub my back and I went nuts."

"What was wrong with rubbing your back?"

"Oh, nothing at all—unless I'm half out of my mind with wanting you—which, of course, I was. But other than that, not one damned thing, I guess."

"I did not try to seduce you, if that's what you think."

"I don't know what I think right now. I just know that I've got to get out of here, and I've got to do it right now."

"But after tomorrow—"

"Don't you see?" he roared. "There isn't going to be any *after tomorrow*. I'm going out there to bang against the wall again—or roast myself in a fireball—or roll end over end down the front straightaway—and you'll be able to hear the fat lady singing clear over here."

"You must have faith that such things won't happen, Ian.

You must have faith in yourself and your abilities."

"Well I don't. And don't you dare try to have faith in me either. I'm not worth it. Every good and decent thing I touch turns directly to shit."

"That's not true."

"It *is* true, Katie." His brittle voice softened and he murmured her name. It was little more than a whisper. "Not Katie. Katriana. My beautiful Katriana." He rolled the word around in his mouth as if to savor the taste it.

He stared at her for countless seconds, then without another word, he opened the door, stepped out into the night, and was gone.

Chapter Ten

If this was love, Katriana wanted no part of it!

She was an *imbécile* to have trusted Ian, or any man. If her own father could barter her away like a cow, how unbelievably foolish she had been to place her trust—and her heart—in the hands of a self-proclaimed scoundrel such as Ian Grayson.

She still had no clue as to what terrible *faux pas* she had committed to bring the fragile walls of their relationship crashing in around her. But for a very few short moments, her world had been right, her husband attentive and responsive, her marriage consummated. Then, in no more than the blink of an eye, everything had disintegrated.

But why?

She spent the remainder of the night huddled in a miserable lump on the tiny sofa beside the front door, the very same place where Ian had made love to her. When he deigned to stomp back through that door, they had much to discuss.

But he didn't come back—stomping, slinking, snarling, apologizing, limping, running, or in any other condition.

Daylight found her alone and confused. The morning marched ever nearer to noon, the hour Ian's race was to begin, and she finally realized that he wasn't coming back. As desperation crept in, she went about fashioning an alternate plan, something she should have done before embarking on this misbegotten journey, both geographical and emotional,

166

with Ian. The possibility of any sort of meaningful relationship between them had been doomed from the start and a savvy person, a woman of the world, would have had a fall back plan in place.

Katriana realized that she wasn't a woman of the world. Making her own way was very difficult. And, oh, God, how it hurt to be abandoned, for no other reason she could find except that she'd neglected to mention she was a virgin.

Ian Grayson apparently didn't care for virgins.

She bathed quickly, keeping in mind Ian's lecture that the hot water in the motor coach was in small supply and must be used sparingly. She was not accustomed to styling her own hair in any sort of extravagant manner, although during the time she had spent with Ian she had mastered the process of shampooing it and blowing it dry. She stood before the mirror in the tiny motor-coach bathroom, fighting tears, and styling her own hair with a diligence born of necessity. The end result was almost pleasing.

She then applied her make-up, dressed in the most exotic and flashy garments she currently owned, and finished with a lavish spritz of her favorite perfume.

She gazed at her reflection in the mirror. Once again the woman staring back at her was undeniably Princess Katriana of Île d'Arinedra. No more disguises. No more hiding. No more Katie Grayson in aviator sunglasses, funny hats, and blue jeans from K-Mart.

No more life with Ian.

That left one final step to put her hastily conceived plan into motion. That last step was straight out the front door.

She strolled boldly through the crowded infield, actively looking for any member of the paparazzi. Yesterday the press had been in a frenzy to interview Ian Grayson's wife on camera. Today they would get their chance. Some lucky reporter was about to find the Runaway Princess and break the story of the decade.

When all that was accomplished, the last step in her plan was to do nothing at all except sit back and wait for her father's men to find her.

Her adventure was over. Her heart was broken.

Princess Katriana was going home.

Detachment. Isolation.

Alone, inside his car . . . inside his driver's helmet . . . his own breathing, surprisingly regular and unhurried, Ian experienced separation from the rest of the world.

Activity buzzed around him, but for these last few minutes before the race commenced, he was alone. He had already belted himself securely into the car and was ready. He recalled even mouthing a few obligatory words for the media. But if asked now to repeat any of those words, he wouldn't have been able to do it. He had no idea what he had said.

Over the two-way radio, his crew chief droned endlessly to somebody about something. The words fed straight into Ian's ears through the earphones clinched there, but it was meaningless chatter, nothing more. If the man happened to be speaking to Ian, he might as well save his breath.

Ian realized that he ought to feel scared, or sick, or something other than numb with shame, but he was unable to drum up any sort of concrete emotion. This almost paralyzing absence of connection with reality was the best he could manage.

In minutes he would race again, tempt Fate, laugh in the face of Danger, hurl his poor not-yet-healed body around the mile-and-a-third Darlington track.

For half a century, people had labeled Darlington "The Track Too Tough to Tame." Some called it "The Lady in

Black." But in Ian's eyes, Darlington was no *lady*. Darlington was a *bitch*—a bitch forever fashioning new and dreadful surprises. If she couldn't sling you into the walls of her treacherous turns, she would settle for chewing up your tires then spitting them out all over the track to trip up another unsuspecting driver.

Today might very well be the day he died, Ian realized. And he couldn't summon up enough emotion to really give a shit.

If the worst happened and this was how it all ended, who—besides Cheryl and her unending quest for more and more alimony—would even miss him? He was a devil of the worst sort.

A taker of virgins.

He winced with shame.

I've got to go back and talk to her—apologize. I've got to make it right, he told himself. But of course he was telling the wrong person. Today he was committed to race. And, God help him, if he didn't manage to hang on and live through the wreck that would surely find him sometime before the day was over, how would Katie ever know that he loved her? Had he bothered to mention that before storming out the door? Had he bothered to apologize for hurting her? For making her first experience with sex an ugly, negative ordeal?

Katie . . . hell, her name wasn't even Katie. It was Katriana. Beautiful, magical, adorable Katriana, who had entrusted herself and her fate to him. And how had he responded to that trust? Used her and cussed her and stormed out in the middle of the night, leaving her alone and unprotected.

Unprotected!

Jesus Christ! The little matter of birth control that he had ignored during last night's sexual fury slammed into him like a bulldozer. The force of it swept his breath away. Sweat dampened his underarms. It rolled down his face. His mouth went dry with shock of it. For a guy with condoms stuck in every damned drawer in the motor coach, he had been remarkably negligent about not putting any of them to use.

"How's the engine sound?" a disembodied voice asked through his earphones.

"Engine? What engine?"

"The damned engine in the damned car that you were supposed to start about half a minute ago when the guy in the suit yelled 'Gentlemen, start your engines.' That's what damned engine." Those words came straight from Benny's mouth, bypassing his crew chief. An owner could grow very testy when his driver wasn't paying attention.

Ian quickly flicked the switch and the engine roared to life. "Sounds fine."

"Jeez," Bennie moaned and then he was gone.

Up ahead of him, Ian saw that the cars had begun to roll, moving off pit road to circle the track for the warm-up laps. He accelerated gently, trailing the car in front of him.

So far . . . so good, he noted to himself. *Not dead yet.*

"What are your temps?"

Ian clamped down hard on his dismay and tried to concentrate on the pre-green-flag rhythms that had been reflex until the last several months. He read aloud over the radio the information from his gauges. He snaked back and forth in the multicolored conga line of cars weaving around the track to build up heat in the tires to generate yet more speed. He'd done all this how many hundreds of times? In every kind of car imaginable, from championship caliber to pieces of crap far worse than his current car. After Daytona, he'd never expected to do any of it again but, by God, here he was.

It takes more than a pile of mangled sheetmetal to stop me, he swore to himself. *I've got to focus on finishing this damned race in one piece, and then I've got to find Katie and apologize.*

The car sounded good. He felt only a few tiny, scattered fingers of anticipation twist through him. The nausea and fear seemed content to stay hidden.

Maybe he could do this. Maybe he could even live through it.

He had to. He wanted to because if he didn't, Katie would never know all that she meant to him. Not that she'd care after what he'd done last night. But it was important to him that she know. What she did with that knowledge would be her decision.

But first he had to get through the race—alive—which would be no small task.

In the middle of the pack of cars, all lined up two by two with military precision, he roared out of Turn Three into and through Turn Four.

This was it. Green flag waving.

"Green, green, green! Go!" his spotter shouted over the radio straight into his ear, as always. So familiar, yet at the same time almost surreal.

"Yeah. I see it," Ian grunted.

He made sure he was past the start-finish line then mashed the gas pedal all the way to the floor and swung out, around, and past the car in front of him, just to show somebody—it didn't really matter who—that he meant business. Just to prove that, at least for today, Ian Grayson was back and might even be a factor.

"Here we go, guys. It's showtime."

"Jeez, even all banged up, you still got it, don'tcha, buddy?" Hank Bottoms, Ian's crew chief, snickered to him over the radio. "By the way, you won't believe what that pretty little wife of yours is doing right now."

Hank's comment startled Ian, breaking his concentration, interrupting his driving rhythm. During a race, Ian and Hank constantly exchanged temperature settings, lap times, technical insights on the car's performance—or, more recently, lack thereof—and how to go from what it was doing to what it should be doing. All this exchange of information took place in short, clipped, curt phrases. Very technical. Very dry. Very necessary. In the middle of a race, they never chatted. Maybe Hank was trying to loosen him up.

Or maybe Hank was trying to tell him something important.

"My wife?"

"Yeah, ya old stud!"

"What about my wife?"

"Hell, she's over by the hauler givin' interviews to the TV people," Hank reported. This time his laugh was more guffaw than chuckle. "Ain't nobody watchin' the race any more. Everybody's watchin' her. Benny's loving it. You know how Benny gets a hard-on any time we get some TV time. Nothing like getting that sponsor's name out there for everybody to see. It's all about sellin' stuff, ain't it?"

Sweltering inside the 120-plus-degree car, Ian felt his blood halt, right before it froze into solid ice. "Somebody get her back inside the motor coach, *now!*" he roared. "Right now! And stay with her. Don't leave her alone for a minute."

"In a sec," Hank promised. "How's your water temp?"

"I mean it!" Ian yelled. "My water temperature is just freakin' ducky right now, but my wife needs some damned help, if you don't mind!"

His answer was a knowing, "guy-to-guy" kind of chuckle.

Trapped inside his car until the end of the race, Ian was helpless to stop what was happening.

Just what the hell was Katie up to now?

He rounded Turn Two, automatically swinging wide, so close to the wall he almost brushed it, building up speed to blast down the back stretch and . . . *there she was* . . . on the huge infield video screen that displayed the network television feed of the race broadcast. Ian seldom even glanced at it unless the cars were slowed for a caution flag. Too distracting. But the face there on this day was Katie's, and it was impossible to ignore.

Aw, hell! No need to fool himself. Katie Grayson didn't even exist. She wasn't a real person. The beautiful lady on the screen was Princess Katriana, in all of her royal splendor—smiling, laughing. Her hair was once again splendid and full, flowing across her shoulders and down her back as she hadn't dared to wear it since the night they left Florida. Her image filled the screen—and his heart. He could swear he heard the ghost of her laughter tinkling through the radio static in his ears. The muscles in his back—and in other, less mentionable places—zinged with the bittersweet memory of her touch.

"I said, somebody get her back in the motor coach," he yelled again.

"You got it, buddy," Hank answered, and with his next breath asked how the tires were reacting to the cloud cover that had drifted over the track.

Ian's back was stiff. His leg throbbed. But he sure as hell wasn't scared any more. He couldn't pay enough attention to his driving to be scared. He stepped up his pace just a touch to get around the track again, and back to those few seconds when he could return his gaze to the video screen. To do that required passing a few cars, but he did it, and he suspected he did it with a flourish. Once upon a time he'd been pretty damned good at passing cars.

173

Katie had made no effort to disguise herself. Had she gone so far as to admit on television who she was? Even if she hadn't, could there be any doubt after that damned interview? Didn't she know the consequences of such foolishness? Did she want her father to find her?

Jesus! Did she hate him that much? Ian wondered. Had he hurt her that badly?

"Hey, Ian. What're we supposed to be calling you now? *Your Highness?*" This time it was Benny himself on the radio.

Ian told him—in one-syllable words—what to do to himself. Benny roared with laughter. "You just keep passing those cars, boy, and I might even try it and let you watch," he answered. "A guy's got to celebrate some way. We common folk don't all have a fancy, royal piece of tail waiting for us at home like you do."

"Celebrate what?"

"*Celebrate what?* Boy, aren't you paying attention? You're in fifth place right now."

Ian's mind was overloaded with problems, but he allowed himself a quick time-out, just long enough for a deep, celebratory breath. He wanted to savor this moment, revel in it, remember it. How long had it been since he'd even cracked the top ten? And now he was running fifth? How had that happened?

"What'd you do, Benny? Put a real engine in it this time?" he joked, trying to conceal the emotion in his voice. Was this an omen that his life might, somehow, get back on track?

"You just drive, boy. I'll have somebody see about your wife." Benny promised. "Hank, get somebody over there to take care of Ian's wife. Okay?"

Ian sighed with relief, held his line on the track, and raced on with a vigor that he hadn't felt in a long time.

He lost track of time, for an hour, certainly—maybe longer.

He dealt with the inevitable wrecks. One was bad and one not so bad. He was amazed that he wasn't involved in either. The bad one happened directly in front of him, giving him no more than a microsecond of reaction time before he shot straight into a solid curtain of smoke, blind to anything in front of him. Two seconds later he roared out the other side of the smokescreen, unscathed, all in one piece, and believing in miracles.

The car was geared all wrong and the restarts ate him alive. On top of that aggravation, the pit stop times were pitifully slow. But he was racing again, and it felt good.

How surprising to feel comfortable again in the car, focused, able to block out everything but the track in front of him, the cars around him, the gauges on his dashboard, the voices on the radio . . . until . . .

Something wasn't right. It gnawed at his subconscious. Something he couldn't quite define.

It took another couple of laps to figure out what had grabbed his attention. Certainly it was no part of the race itself, and it wasn't his car. Other than the bad choice of gearing, this was the best car Bennie had put under him in years.

Something about the infield. Something not quite right.

With each lap, he shot quick glances toward the little bits of the infield he could see flashing past him. People, pits, car haulers, campers, motor homes. Nothing out of the ordinary. Katie's beautiful face no longer graced the large video screen. She was safely back in the motor coach, or maybe the lounge in the car-hauler, with her impromptu bodyguard from Benny's crew.

Nothing on the track. Nothing in the infield.

He glanced up. And spied a helicopter hovering low over the infield. Then slowly it began descending. Medical helicopters sometimes took off during a race, but he'd never seen one *arrive* in the middle of a race.

"What's the deal with the helicopter?" he asked over the radio, almost afraid to hear the answer.

"Don't know," Hank answered. "Somebody on the field frequency sure is all stirred up over it. No permission to land or something like that. A bunch of security guys are on the way over there now, I think. Why?"

"Just curious," he muttered. Then, "Who's with my wife?" A bolt of pure sexual thrill ran through him as he pronounced those words, *my wife*. It felt good. Hell, it felt *damned* good.

No answer.

"I said, who's with my wife?"

Still no answer, then a soft, apologetic, "Shit."

"You didn't send anybody, did you?"

"We got busy. Sorry about that."

In the space of a heartbeat, Ian went from totally focused on the race to almost nonfunctioning. "Hank, if anything happens to her, I'll kill you. I promise I will," he spat through his clenched teeth.

"What could happen to her?"

He didn't trust himself to answer. He couldn't see exactly where the helicopter had landed in the infield, but having watched it descend, he had a fair idea where he could find it.

On the very next lap, as he rounded Turn Three, he dropped his car low on the track and roared down the pit lane—much, much faster than the allowed speed limit.

"What the hell are you doing?" Hank screamed at him. "What's wrong?"

"You better tell anybody in my way to get the hell out of it, 'cause I'm not slowing down for anything or anybody.'"

"Ian, have you lost your damned mind?" Benny yelled into the radio.

"Not yet."

"Then you better get your butt back out on the track, you—" A serendipitous burst of static masked Benny's descriptive name for Ian. "—or you're *fired.*"

"It's been fun," Ian muttered as he took the sharp left-turn into the infield from the pit lane, tires squealing in protest, people jumping and scattering out of his way, as he plowed through.

He was going much too fast, but that was just too damned bad. He streaked his way around the infield area until he found the helicopter. Its blades were rotating, building speed for liftoff.

He had one shot at it.

Never lifting his foot from the gas, he aimed the car straight at the front of the helicopter, the place he could do the most damage to the machine but not to the people inside.

He said a quick prayer for Katie because there was no doubt that she was inside that helicopter, as well as for his own black heart and empty soul, if he managed to screw up and hurt somebody . . . kill himself . . .

The chatter in his ears was deafening. The words all ran together in a stream of profanity.

His constant nightmare since the wreck at Daytona rushed head-on to meet him. It wasn't the concrete wall he had dreamed of. This time it was a machine of metal and glass and whirling blades. At the moment, a stationary concrete wall would have been a lot less fearsome.

There was a shriek of metal striking metal. The car crashed, crumpled—as did the front of the helicopter—then stopped. In the seconds of shocked silence that followed, Ian keyed his mike, "Hey, thanks for all the help, guys, but never mind. I just took care of if myself."

Wham!

Something large and substantial—and vicious—rammed full-bore into the front of the helicopter, and drove it reeling backward on its skids.

Katriana's head had been aching abominably, and now this awful, sickening, tilting thud.

Would this godforsaken day ever end? Was it not enough that she'd been forced to deal with reporters? Smile and laugh through her heartache and pretend to be the perfect little princess in front of all those television cameras, all the time hoping and praying that someone, somewhere would see her and come to take her home?

But did that "someone" have to be her father himself?

Prince Henri, the ruling monarch of Île d'Arinedra, with his ever-present entourage of meaty bodyguards who could easily tear a man apart with their bare hands—why were *all of them* here? Could he not have sent someone with a bit of compassion, someone with a handy shoulder and a spare handkerchief? Someone who wouldn't berate a princess with a broken heart for crying?

Prince Henri carried his slight, compact form with rigid military inflexibility, although instead of the full dress uniform he often found so impressive and necessary, he was dressed in a gray business suit matching exactly to the gunmetal gray of his hair and eyebrows. Those bushy eyebrows were currently draped low and furious over his steely eyes. His thin, almost lipless mouth slashed across his face, drawn and pinched into a cruel line.

Prince Henri was *not* in a good mood.

He'd spent the last several minutes firing rude and intrusive questions nonstop at Katriana. Mercifully, his staccato inquisition ceased with the collision, but he quickly shifted his bellowing to a string of curses that were almost comical when pronounced in his aristocratic French. She had never heard her father utter such profanities.

She made a show of ignoring him and his boorish behavior as she tried to peer over the back of the front seat and out the cracked windshield of the craft, now tilted from the impact. A crowd of fans and media was gathering quickly around the wounded helicopter.

The pilot cut the power immediately after impact, allowing the whooshing blades to slow and then stop altogether, before he leaped from the aircraft to assess the damage.

In the sudden, almost deafening, silence, Katriana turned back to her father, only to be greeted by stony hostility flashing from his eyes, as black as the succulent olives of Greece. Her overloaded brain registered that a few of his iron gray hairs were out of place. That was as mussed as Katriana had ever known him to be.

"How many ways do you intend to embarrass me, Katriana?" he challenged her, his thin lips barely moving as he pronounced the words. "You have many things to clarify."

She opened her mouth to respond, but before she could utter a word, a familiar voice from somewhere just outside the helicopter interrupted, insinuating itself between her and her angry father, causing her disobedient heart to jump in surprised joy.

"I'd like to talk to my wife for a minute, if that's all right with everybody," that loud voice insisted. Despite his choice of words, it was clear from his tone that Ian Grayson was issuing an edict, not requesting permission.

179

"Sit still," her father instructed her. "I will deal with this cretin."

"He's not a cretin," Katriana snapped. "He's an exceedingly . . ."

"Silence, Katriana."

But Ian refused to be denied. "My wife, please," he shouted. "I know she's in there."

Her father blasted her with another black and icy stare as with furious and jerky movements, he unfastened his seatbelt. He stood up and tugged his cuffs to ensure that each with its respective solid gold link was perfectly positioned, then ducked his head and, preceded by his guards, stepped from the helicopter on to the ground. His men arranged themselves around him.

"Young man," Prince Henri intoned in his most fearsome and imperious voice, the one that could send even the adult Katriana scurrying for cover, "you have destroyed this helicopter."

"They make 'em every day," Ian fired back. He sounded quite unimpressed that the ruler of Île d'Arinedra was conducting a personal conversation with him. "I'm sure you can find a new one."

The guards bristled, and Katriana saw each of them lower a hand to his concealed weapon.

Peering through the helicopter's side door through which her father had just exited, she could see Ian. He'd crawled from his wrecked car. He stood bold and defiant, face-to-face with her father—much taller and stronger than Prince Henri—and quite overwhelmingly male in his white, black and orange driver's suit. He was every bit as angry the prince.

"Why have you attempted to assassinate us?" her father demanded.

Ian drew a steadying breath. "Sir, if I'd seriously tried to kill you, I suspect you'd be dead right now, not standing here talking about it."

Katriana could not conceive of her father allowing anyone to speak to him in such a way, but long seconds passed and he had not yet demanded that his bodyguards draw their weapons and execute Ian on the spot. Perhaps there was hope.

But Ian showed no fear. "I apologize for wrecking your helicopter, but my time—and my wife—were running out and so were my choices."

"The helicopter does not belong to me, young man. It belongs to a friend, and you've damaged it so severely that it is now unserviceable." Her father appeared to be readying himself for battle and, true to form, was more concerned about the condition of the helicopter than he was about her.

"Have your friend contact me. I'm sure we can work it out like gentlemen." Ian shrugged as if it scarcely mattered to him. "I don't have a daughter to offer him in payment of the debt, but we can explore other alternatives. Again, like gentlemen." Ian used careful emphasis each time he spoke the word *gentlemen*.

Although, Ian's tone and demeanor indicated nothing less than respect, her father's face commenced to blotch, flushing such a vivid red as to approach purple.

"Ian, you mustn't—" she cautioned, sliding across her father's empty seat, then out of the helicopter and on to the ground.

"Stay inside, Katriana," her father roared.

"Non, Papa," she declared, amazing herself with her own impertinence. She faced Ian. "What is the meaning of this?"

"The meaning of this," Ian took pains to emphasize her exact words as he repeated them, "is that I think you owe me the courtesy of telling me just what the hell is going on here."

"Let it go, Ian," she said. "Just let it go and everything will be all right again."

"Let what go?"

"Me. It. All of it. Everything. I've made a terrible mistake pretending to be something I'm not. I must go back to where I should have been all the time, and everything will be right again."

"Everything . . . will . . . be . . . right . . . again?" Ian repeated. He seemed unable to make sense of those few simple words.

"*Oui.*"

"God help us both, Katriana," he murmured. His voice dropped low, husky. His whole body trembled with emotion. The words were barely discernible, yet each one ripped through her as if shot from a rifle. "How is your leaving me going to make anything right ever again?"

The crowd of curious fans and journalists crushed closer around them, focusing on every word, every movement unfolding in front of them. Ian stood before them all, so brave, unconcerned that he was baring his heart not just to her, but to the entire world.

"Don't I get a chance to make it right?" he asked, his voice cracking. "To apologize for my stupid behavior? To apologize for last night, for God's sake?"

She couldn't bear it. She could not bear the ache that rose from every part of her as she witnessed his distress. "Why are you doing this, Ian? Why are you making it so hard for me?"

"God, Katie, don't you realize that I don't want to make anything in your life more difficult? All I want is another chance to try to make you happy. I want us to start over and pretend that last night didn't happen."

"Ian, please don't—" she implored him, embarrassed. How could he ignore their huge audience? How could he share so casually something so intimate with these people clustered around them? She had no doubt that every sordid detail would be reported on the evening news, then again in tomorrow morning's newspaper. She shuddered.

"Not here, Ian. Not like this," she begged. "Please."

"OK, you tell me when and where," he demanded. "I'll be sure to be there—but will you? Stupid me!" He slapped his hand against his forehead. "I could have sworn that you were trying to leave."

"Well, I was. Of course, I was—until—" she gestured toward the wrecked car speared on the front of the helicopter. "Why on earth did you do that?"

"I ran out of options, Katie, and I couldn't let you leave without saying good-bye. I had to stop you long enough so I could at least tell how much I love you. And I had to apologize."

"Apologize?" she repeated. Then she lost that train of thought as the word *love* grabbed her attention, roaring through her like a flow of lava. She let it go where it would for the simple reason that she had no defenses to subdue it. She allowed it to bubble around inside of her until it lodged in a deep and secret place where she could clutch it close and savor the sound and the feel of it.

He loved her!

"For last night," he answered. "For the things I said. For what I did."

"Ian!" she admonished, trying once again to direct his attention to the crowd gathered around them, the television cameras aimed straight at them.

He shrugged. "Hell, by now I guess they all know what a son of a bitch I am."

His answer from the crowd was a handful of uncomfortable chuckles, some foot shuffling, one soft *You da man, Ian,* from near the back, followed by a smattering of applause.

"Well, I *am* a son of a bitch," he said. "I swear to God, Katie, that I love you, and what did I do? I treated you badly. You're gentle, beautiful, and innocent, and I—well, let's just say that I'm not any of those things. I couldn't recognize the goodness and decency in you because I don't know anything about those things. I don't understand them. I accused you of actions and motives that you aren't capable of feeling."

"Ian, please don't," she begged of him. "You mustn't—"

"You're wrong about that, Katie," he murmured. "Because, yes, I must. I've told the truth. What I said and did was a disgrace to the beautiful and wonderful woman that you are. I love you, Katie Grayson—I love you a lot—more than I can put into words. I did what I had to do here today because I knew damned well that you were leaving me, and I couldn't allow that to happen."

"Katriana, come. I'm tired of this. We must make other arrangements," Prince Henri spoke, ordering her in the same dominant tone he used to address his horse. Katriana recalled him showing more kindness to his dogs than he was now extending to her. Yet another humiliation in a day chock-full of humiliations.

In the brief instant between one heartbeat and the next, she realized that her decision to go to or stay was no decision at all.

It had already been made.

Perhaps late one evening outside a public restroom somewhere in South Georgia as Ian had carefully watched over her.

Or maybe while shopping in that K-Mart in Atlanta as he introduced her to a slice of Americana.

More probably, before either of those things occurred, she had already fallen in love with Ian Grayson. Could one fall in love over a baked potato, a burrito and a bottle of beer? Or while watching a video of a car wreck?

Impossible to choose one defining moment, because each memory of their brief time together was tightly woven with all the others into the fabric of her love for him.

"*Papa,*" she said, turning to face her father, "make whatever arrangements you must make, but I will not be leaving with you. I'm staying here with my husband."

"What nonsense, Katriana," Prince Henri barked. She knew that tone very well. He was growing impatient with this turn of events. "Have you learned nothing from this unfortunate escapade?"

"I've learned that I love my husband and that he loves me. And for now, that's enough."

"I have no doubt that your marriage is nothing but a farce. And so is your husband. You're now the laughing stock of the world. Do you realize that?"

"You are wrong about all of those things, Papa," she said. "But even if any or all of them should prove to be true, I don't care. It doesn't matter."

"Our marriage is legal, sir," Ian interrupted. "You can rest assured that your daughter is my wife in every possible way."

Prince Henri turned his furious gaze toward Ian. "I am properly addressed as Your Highness," he instructed.

She watched Ian consider her father's imperious words, then relax and allowed himself to smile. It was an impertinent, almost brash smile. She wanted to savor that smile, but instead she braced herself for what surely would follow.

"This is not your country, sir, and we don't bow to royalty here," Ian said, with no pretense of a polite preamble. "What you are is my father-in-law, and for that reason alone I owe you respect and my gratitude that you fathered Katriana and helped her become the beautiful, wonderful woman she is today."

Ian's brash smile faded away and was replaced by a hint of grudging respect. "Understand, sir, that I'll do everything in my power to take care of her and make her happy, and have no doubt in this world that I'll love her. One day, for her sake, you and I will be obliged to resolve our differences, but today isn't that day."

Prince Henri stared at Ian for a long moment, unblinking and silent. "You are quite ill-mannered, young man."

Katriana moved toward her father, to try to explain. "*Papa,* you do not understand—"

"Silence, please," he instructed, then turned his attention again to Ian. "I understand that you enjoy a certain amount of *célébrité* in this country."

"*Papa—,*" she began again, but once more he silenced her.

"I would hope he can speak for himself, Katriana."

"That I can do, sir," Ian was quick to respond.

"And you are financially secure?"

"More or less." Ian shifted his weight slightly, causing Katriana to wonder if he had reinjured his leg or back in his mad crash into the helicopter.

"Do you believe that you can support Katriana in the style to which she has been accustomed all of her life?"

Ian seemed amused. "Not a chance."

Prince Henri almost allowed himself a smile. Or perhaps it was a grimace. Katriana was having difficulty determining the difference between the two. Conducting such a personal conversation with a commoner was out of character for her father.

"From the previous exchange between you and Katriana, I must infer that your marriage has been consummated."

Katriana sighed, flushing with embarrassment. Why did these two men insist on discussing the most intimate of subjects before a crowd of so many onlookers? She was humiliated.

"You may assume whatever you want to assume," Ian answered. "I doubt that this is the time or the place to discuss such a private matter."

"Young man, I am finding this situation difficult enough, so watch your manners."

Ian appeared undisturbed at the chastisement.

Katriana mused that while Ian's behavior was surprisingly civil, her father was the one appeared ill-bred and offensive. Was this absurd situation bringing out his worst traits, or was he always so odious? Katriana looked at her father for the first time with clear and unclouded eyes. She didn't like the man she saw.

"My point in asking these questions," Prince Henri continued, "is to determine if you are capable of fathering a child."

Katriana watched those unexpected words catch Ian unawares, as nothing else in the conversation had yet done. "I know of no reason why I can't," he answered, then frowned as if he perhaps regretted favoring Prince Henri with an answer.

"I hope you understand that I ask this question for a reason. As I am sure you know, Katriana was betrothed. But now that marriage will not occur, even though her betrothed is my old and trusted friend."

"I have heard that story, sir. She was so excited over marrying your old and trusted friend that she left everything she'd known in her life and ran away." He stopped, searching for the right words. "I love Katriana. And I can only imagine the pain and unhappiness that drove her to run away."

"I find this conversation distasteful." Her father

187

attempted to steer the conversation in another direction.

"And I find *that* entire situation distasteful."

Did Ian not realize he was treading on dangerous ground? He didn't seem to care.

"If that is supposed to disturb me, it does not," Prince Henri stated. "However, the point I was attempting to make before this conversation strayed, was that Katriana's prospects of ever marrying into any of the noble houses of Europe are now ruined. In fact, she now seems to dwell in a grim no-man's-land. Although your government recognizes her marriage to you, the Church does not. If there is any chance that a child has been or will be conceived, then I shall be forced to put my distress at this union aside and instruct the Vatican to immediately commence the process."

Oh, *mon dieu*. Katriana's heart fluttered, as if it were trying to break free from her chest. Ian would not care for *that*. She would have to pull him aside, in private, and explain to him what was required, what must be done before—

"Excuse me," Ian spoke up. To her dismay, she knew what words he would utter before he spoke them. "I don't understand what the Vatican has to do with any of this."

Yes, those were the words.

"Do you think I have not researched your heritage, young man?" her father snapped. "Do you think that I am such a simpleton that I would accept you at face value into my family without knowing your past? Without knowing that you were previously married?"

"You didn't even know who I was until a couple of hours ago, and I have some doubts that you'll ever accept *me* into your family."

"I have very competent and speedy sources," her father continued, ignoring Ian's last few words. "And one of the bits of information derived from those sources has brought to my attention the necessity of working with the Vatican to arrange for the annulment of your previous marriage."

"Now, just wait a minute. I won't allow that!"

"The Church will not recognize Katriana's marriage to a divorced man. It is as simple as that."

"Well, that's unfortunate, but my church *will* recognize it, so it looks like Katie may have to change churches."

"I assure you, the annulment will not be a difficulty. My staff will make all the necessary arrangements. You need do nothing at all."

"I must insist that no one attempt to alter even one tiny grain of my past, especially my first marriage. Who are you to say it never happened. Of course Cheryl and I were married. I realize your faith gives you that option, and I have to respect that. But my faith doesn't, and it's my past that's on the chopping block.

"Sir, I love Katriana and will do anything I can to make her happy, but that's one thing I can't do. And I absolutely refuse to be manipulated that way. My past is what it is and that's the way it will stay. That marriage was by no means perfect, but Cheryl and I were married for twelve years and beneath all that pain and bitterness are some very nice memories. It's my history, and even you, sir, can't change history."

Ian's hands clenched into fists, which he was wise enough to leave at his sides. Electricity seemed to hum from his body and Katriana suspected that deep within him, he was battling. Throughout that inner struggle, Ian stood still, no part of him moving except for one lone muscle flexing in his jaw.

Prince Henri raised his hands in the eternal Gallic gesture of dismay. "You are much too opinionated and argumentative to conduct business with. I wash my hands of this entire matter. Come, Katriana. We shall call for a car and leave this place."

"Not while they're still racing around the track, you won't," Ian muttered.

"*Papa,* have you not listened to a word either of us has said?" Katriana demanded. She began ticking off, one by one the specific points she aimed to impress on him. "I am an adult. I am an American citizen. I am not leaving here with you. And, *Papa,* although I have been raised to believe otherwise, I cannot insist that Ian disavow his previous marriage. He is adamant that he will not permit an annulment, and I trust that he has a good reason for such strong feelings. The Church may never recognize that I am married to him, but in my own heart I know I am. Perhaps one day he will feel differently about this but for now, I must, and will, support his decision. I am Ian's wife, *Papa,* and I will stay here with him, under any condition, even this one. Do you understand what I am saying?"

"I understand your words, Katriana, but not your choice. When the babies come and you realize you are not married in the eyes of the Church, what will you do then?"

Her heart swelled and she felt that the proper words might have been waiting there forever, just so she could answer this one question, perhaps the most important one of her life. "I shall love them with all my heart. I shall try to instill in them all of the virtues my father instilled into me. And when they are old enough, I shall pack them up and take them to visit their *grand-père* in his beautiful palace that overlooks the sea."

For the first time since the poor, now-crushed helicopter landed in the infield and her father stepped from it to accompany her home, his eyes softened. The rigid lines around his mouth relaxed. Prince Henri of Île d'Arinedra could indeed smile. Katriana had seen him do it on rare occasions. And she watched him smile then.

If he had been any other man in the world, she might have taken the drop of moisture at the corner of his eye as a sign of emotion. But this was her father, and such tenderness was not possible.

"And their *grand-père* shall indeed be waiting for them, counting the days," he responded with an unexpected, bewildering gentleness. "Beyond that I can make no promises."

The unprecedented softening lasted for very few seconds, then was gone. His Royal Highness Prince Henri was back in character. His back was once again ramrod straight. His head angled back at a precise military tilt. Katriana had long suspected that his perfect posture was intended to give a man of his average height the illusion of a few added inches.

He and his cluster of bodyguards turned as one unit and walked away.

Why would the frightening crowd not disburse?

Katriana was ready to wilt, yet the immense crowd of onlookers and paparazzi stayed as if rooted to the ground, craving even more. Would these people never be satisfied? Was it not sufficient that the most private and delicate elements of Katriana's life, and Ian's, had just been stripped bare and laid at their feet?

She was afraid she might cry even though crying, especially public crying, was forbidden.

She looked down and away from the people surrounding her, closing in on her. She squeezed her eyes shut to block out the onlookers and hold in the tears. Had she made the right decision? Ian had fought for her, but could she trust his words? Could she really trust anything about him? She found him so difficult to understand. Their cultures were so dissimilar.

Although he had made a point of saying lovely words

about his feelings for her, even declaring to the world that he loved her, how could she be sure he wanted her to stay? What did love mean to a man like Ian Grayson? And how did his refusal to annul his first marriage fit into the vicissitudes of their relationship?

"You're not gonna faint on me, are you, Princess?"

Katriana opened her eyes, looked up. Ian was there, in front of her, squinting against the intensity of the South Carolina sun, flashing his dimples and his outrageous smile for the world to see.

She'd heard no sound to indicate that he was there. But with so much shuffling and muttering around her, it came as no surprise that he'd approached without her notice. He could have thundered through the crowd riding on a buffalo and she doubted she could have heard him over the noise, or through her own near-panic.

"*Non.* At least I don't think so."

"Well, just to be sure, how 'bout a lift?"

With no more warning than those few words, he swept her up off her feet and lifted her high in his arms, cradling her against his chest. It was heady and thrilling. Only moments ago she was fighting tears but now she laughed out loud with the sudden joy of being held by him.

Until she remembered his injuries.

"Ian, your back! Your leg! You mustn't . . ."

"Hush. My back and my leg are just fine. And, later on if they're not, then maybe you can rub 'em for me. You do that very well, you know." He spoke low and only for her to hear.

She buried her face in his neck. He smelled of sweat and heat and sunshine. She was anxious that after all she'd endured that day she too might smell much the same way.

For shame, she chided herself. A princess never sweats.

But Katie Grayson can. And did. And would.

She giggled.

"What's that all about?" Ian asked.

"I was thinking about sweat."

"Are you allowed to think about sweat?" he teased. "I seem to remember that organs and bodily functions are off limits. And sweat is definitely a bodily function."

"As of this moment, I shall think about and discuss anything I care to, including sweat," she declared. "In fact, I will even announce to the world that I am presently sweating."

"In public? For shame, Princess Katriana."

"Don't you see, Ian? Princess Katriana would never in a million years countenance sweat, even on a blistering hot day like today. Ah, but this Katie Grayson girl, she is another creature entirely. She does all sorts of outrageous things. She sweats if she wants to. She wears boots when she goes dancing. She even eats chicken with her fingers."

"I heard a rumor that she was seen in public wearing— excuse me, this is too horrible to believe—*clothes off the rack.*" Ian rolled is eyes in mock dismay. "Of course, I never pay any attention to rumors, but . . ."

"You are exceedingly naughty, I think," she chastised him, aiming a playful swat at his arm.

"And you, Mrs. Princess Katie Grayson with beads of sweat on your nose, are exceedingly beautiful."

She flushed with pleasure at his outrageous flattery, but maintained enough presence of mind to murmur, "We must look ridiculous," as a smattering of applause at Ian's bold compliment broke out from the people close enough to have heard it.

"No, we don't. We look spontaneous and romantic. And I can assure you that I personally look gallant as hell." He turned, still cradling her close, and started making his way through the crowd toward the motor coach. "Richard Gere did this at the end of a movie once. Chicks love it."

"So does this make me a chick?"

"I doubt it." He angled them through the murmuring crowd, which cooperated and parted for them. "I'm a married man now. I don't hang out with chicks any more. My wife won't let me."

She laughed again, reveling in the delight of his teasing.

Their warm intimacy, even amidst the crush of bodies closed in around them, was shattered by a lone voice calling out from deep in the crowd. "So when can we have an in-depth interview with both of you?"

Ian turned, following the sound of that disembodied voice, trying to put a face to it as he peered into the heart of the mob. "We'll be around after the race, I'm sure," he called back. "Just look for us. But right now, I need to get cleaned up."

"Maybe just a few words?" the reporter countered.

Ian sighed. "No, not now," then muttered a few words under his breath about reporters.

"What does *pushy-assed* mean?" she whispered, drawing her mouth close enough to his ear to be heard.

He chuckled out loud then answered also in an intimate whisper, "Don't worry about it. I doubt there's a French equivalent."

His march through the crowd soon ended at the gate leading into the drivers' private camping compound. The guard stationed there recognized Ian immediately and was quick to let them pass through. He shut the gate with obvious pleasure in the faces of the reporters trying to crowd through close behind them.

"Thanks. I owe you one," Ian threw over his shoulder as he tramped on toward his motor coach, still carrying her as if she were made of feathers. "By the way, if you catch any of those guys trying to storm the castle, this genuine, full-blooded princess I'm carrying around in my arms says, 'Off with their heads.' "

The guard's belly laugh trailed them all the way down the walkway to the front door of Ian's coach. Huge, immaculate, shiny camping vehicles such as Ian's lined both sides of the walkway, all standing silent and at attention, their occupants engaged in either actual racing on the track or watching their husbands and fathers race.

Some of the vehicles sported awnings to shade their doorways and windows. Others had long wooden tables and cushioned chairs arranged outside their front doors. Children's riding toys were scattered about the miniscule strips of ground surrounding many of them, as they sat side by side in their silent splendor. The setting was idyllic, broken only by the rumbling thunder of racecars still dashing around the track at breakneck speed.

So this would be how she would live large chunks of her life, traveling from track to track with Ian, living in his motor coach, becoming friends with his friends. Next year at this time, would she be comfortable and settled into her new life? She felt confident that she would, eager to jump in and get started.

She did admit to a touch of anxiety at some of the unfamiliar intricacies, the minutiae of living as a commoner, she was bound to encounter. For instance, perfecting proper usage of a toothpick. How did one perform the required function, whatever it might be, in one's mouth with a pointed sliver of wood yet not puncture one's tender gum tissues? And why?

She had much to learn, but, oh my, what a magnificent teacher to instruct her in all that she needed to know.

"We might have a slight problem." Ian broke through her musings. "I suppose you didn't think to lock the front door when you left this morning, did you?"

"Lock the front door?"

"I'm guessing that means no. Actually, I'm *hoping* that means no, because I don't have the key with me."

She sighed, wondering if she would ever become accustomed to the simple, ordinary things that everyone else took for granted. Things like locking doors, and carrying around keys for unlocking them. "I'll get better with practice, I'm certain," she said.

"No problem. Don't worry about it. It's not nearly as complicated as using a can opener." He winked, and unlatched the door. "Anybody who drives a five-speed Porsche as well as you do won't have a problem learning about door keys."

"In the meantime . . ." he angled them through the narrow opening and up the entryway steps. "Welcome home, Katie Grayson. I have a much finer home in North Carolina, but this little threshold will have to be the one you get carried over."

"Is this some sort of American custom?"

"Oh, yes, indeed, Mrs. Grayson, a very important one. You're not officially married until you get carried across the threshold."

"Well, I do want to be officially married."

"And now you are."

He deposited her carefully on the couch and she flushed with the memory of what had occurred between them there, on that same couch, the night before. She focused back on those moments, trying to recapture all the heady sensations, the fire that Ian had kindled in her. The touch of his hands exploring her body. His quick intake of breath, the groans he tried to stifle, as she dared to return those intimate touches.

The wild, tumbling assault on her senses as he introduced her to the physical act of love.

The devastation that enveloped her when he slammed the door behind him as he left and walked away.

Ian sat down beside her, all the laughter and teasing fading from his eyes, replaced by a deeper, more intense emotion.

"You stood up for me, Katie. Your father pointed out all the things that are wrong with me, yet you still chose me over everything you have ever known in your life. That amazes me. What possessed you to do that? Why would you do such a thing for me?"

"I didn't do it for you, Ian. I did it for me. I did it because I love you. I had no other choice. After knowing you and living with you, even for such a short time, I could not have gone back to my other life. After being with you, knowing the way love should be between a man and a woman, I could never have endured marriage to Sir Christian. Ugh." She made a face.

"Are princesses allowed to say 'ugh'?" His wonderful mouth, the mouth that could kiss her senseless and turn her to a bubbling, seething mass of lava, curled up in a smile.

"No," she admitted. "But sometimes they do."

"I hope you never say 'ugh' about me."

"I cannot imagine doing that."

"Katie, let's be serious for a minute. I'm not easy to live with. I'm spoiled and indulged by the press and my fans and the people who work with me. I have an ego the size of this motor coach, yet everybody around me excuses my bad behavior because they're paid to keep me happy. I'm cranky when I don't get my way. I'm used to being the center of attention. I'm demanding. And I've been told that I snore."

"You do snore."

"But, Katie, please try to remember when I'm doing all of

those things and you want to kick my butt, that I love you and I want to make our marriage work. I know how scared you are. Right now everything is strange and frightening. But whenever you feel afraid, just remember that I'm afraid too. I'm so afraid I'll mess it up again like I did my first marriage. I'm not sure I even know how to be married. Everything I did the first time was wrong."

"Surely not everything. You refused to allow that marriage to be annulled. You promised my father you would do anything to make me happy, except that. Then you mentioned your memories. I found that very touching, Ian. And quite sad."

"Your father didn't."

"Nothing softens my father. He's a strict, unyielding man. He will never understand why you will not agree to renounce your first marriage. But I do."

"Well, I'd appreciate it if you'd explain it to me, because even though it seemed to make sense at the time, I'm not sure I understand it either."

"Because, above all, you are an honest man. And a loyal one."

He gave every appearance of chuckling, except his eyes. His lips smiled. His throat rumbled as he laughed although, to be honest, it sounded forced. But his eyes refused to participate in any part of it. They remained serious and probing, exploring her own with enough intensity to touch her soul. "I've been called lots of things but I don't recall *honest* and *loyal* being found on that list."

"Then you should ignore what those people say. You should listen to me."

"Yes, ma'am." He executed a casual salute.

"You make a joke, Ian, but I found out today how honest and loyal you are. You refused to let me leave. You risked everything that means anything to you, your career, your health, everything. And you did it in front of the paparazzi and the entire world. But the most incredible part is that you did it for *me*. No one has ever risked anything at all for me. When you shouted out that you love me, I wanted to jump and dance. I wanted to fly."

"I do love you, Katie, and I had to tell you. I couldn't let you go. You're a part of me. Like my leg or my arm. Like my heart."

"And so is she, Ian. So is your first wife. She is part of you and you can't let her go either. You shouldn't have to."

"It's not like that at all, Katie. That's been over for years. Whatever is left is ugly. Nothing but a big, bleeding sore of disappointment and anger."

"And memories, Ian. Those memories that you want to hold on to are left too."

He took some seconds to consider what she had said then nodded. "Maybe."

"For sure, Ian. Not maybe."

"So what does that have to do with anything?"

"It has to do with the kind of man you are, the kind of man I have married and will live with for all of my life, the man who will be the father of my children. Not only do I love you, Ian, I respect you. I want to learn to be like you, the kind of person who doesn't run from problems but chooses to face them head-on, running them down in a racecar, battering into them so they can't fly away and turn into history before they are addressed."

"That's a lot of faith to place in a guy you barely know. I swear to God that I'll try as hard as I can to be all that you deserve, Katriana, but that's a tall order. You may have to settle for something less."

"Well, there *is* your snoring problem." She needed to

lighten the moment or she would surely cry. Whether from joy or love or just plain needing to cry, she had no idea. She wasn't yet familiar enough with crying to be acquainted with all the various reasons to do it.

"See what I've done to you? You're turning into quite a little tease, aren't you?"

"Do you not think I know English well enough to know what a *tease* really is?"

"Well, you're a little bit of that too, but that's not always a bad thing. In fact, I'd be delighted to act right now on that aspect of your teasing and start off by kissing you on your pretty little mouth and a few other interesting and selected places, but I'm too sweaty to smell like anything you'd want to kiss."

"We both sweat like commoners, don't we?" When had sweating become such a delightful activity? Her father would be appalled. The nuns would be appalled. By all rights, she should be appalled by her own shameless behavior. But she wasn't. She was elated by it.

"That's easily remedied, right down that hall in the shower," Ian noted. Then as any self-respecting rogue would do—and Ian Grayson was a devilish rogue indeed—he arched an eyebrow and inquired, "Would you care to join me?"

"It's so tiny. Surely there isn't room for two."

"Well, Katie Grayson, I'm not saying there is and I'm not saying there isn't. All I'm saying is there's only one way to find out."